MUMMY'S *the* WORD

Jan Fields

Annie's®
AnniesFiction.com

Books in the Museum of Mysteries series

Library of Congress-in-Publication Data
Mummy's the Word / by Jan Fields
p. cm.
I. Title
2021947117

AnniesFiction.com
(800) 282-6643
Museum of Mysteries™
Series Creators: Shari Lohner and Lorie Jones
Series Editor: Lorie Jones

10 11 12 13 14 | Printed in China | 9 8 7 6 5 4 3 2 1

1

Perched on a slight rise on the California coast near Monterey, the Reed Museum of Art and Archaeology offered magnificent views of the Pacific Ocean. Visitors who walked the well-manicured grounds could hear the crash of the waves and smell the briny water.

From the outside, the museum resembled a ritzy Spanish-revival mansion or the courthouse it had once been. Inside, the elaborate ceilings and spectacular views competed with an incredible collection of art and artifacts gathered from all over the world. Scarlett McCormick had seen larger collections but few more impressive.

As with its beautiful collection, the museum wasn't the largest Scarlett had ever seen. It wasn't even the largest she'd ever worked in. But some days it felt massive, an overwhelming responsibility that rested on her shoulders as brand-new curator and poked every fear of failure she'd ever had.

Sometimes Scarlett could transform her anxiety into excitement by viewing her new job as an adventure. She'd pursued adventure on digs as an archaeologist, and now she was tackling the adventure of tending this amazing place and the collection it housed.

Though Scarlett had held the job as head curator of the museum for only a few weeks, she already loved the place. The museum had been founded a dozen years before, but the building had stood in the exact same spot in Crescent Harbor since 1927. It even had its own clock tower with a spiral staircase that led to a truly breathtaking view. Whenever possible, Scarlett made a point of ascending the stairs and soaking in the power of the view. The strenuous climb had the added bonus of serving as her aerobics for the day.

The contents of the museum, originating in ancient Greece, Rome, Egypt, the Far East, and more, had all been collected by the man who'd founded the museum, tech billionaire and philanthropist Devon Reed.

The ancient artifacts in the collection had led Devon to offer the position to Scarlett, or so he'd told her on the phone during her unusual interview process. In truth, she'd never met the man. She'd been told the hiring had to be done through phone interviews and emails because the billionaire was rarely in one place for long.

Now, she was eager to meet the elusive Devon and learn what he was like in person. The opportunity would finally come in the next few days. So far, she had no idea when his actual arrival would occur, and that was only one of the mysteries plaguing her at the moment.

Another sat right in the middle of the antique mahogany desk in her office. Scarlett snatched up the small florist card and reread the neatly printed hieroglyphics.

Usurper.

What did I usurp? It wasn't the first time she'd asked herself that question. The card was an exact match to two other florist cards already in her desk drawer.

Scarlett had one card for each of the weeks she'd worked at the museum. When she'd received the first bloodred bouquet, she'd expected whoever was sending the cards to tire of the sport rather quickly. After all, roses were expensive. She tapped the card against the thumbnail on her left hand. She had to admire this person's dedication to a prank, even a truly creepy one like this.

A sharp rap on her door made her jump. Scarlett dropped the card on the desk, then spun around to face Allie Preston.

"Sorry," Allie said with a grin. "I didn't mean to scare you."

Allie managed Burial Grounds, the museum's coffee shop, when she wasn't surfing or taking photographs. She was born and raised in California, and she had the free spirit to prove it. Allie's sun-bleached light-brown hair sometimes made people underestimate her, but Scarlett knew her friend was as intelligent as she was bold.

Allie raised a cup that was imprinted with the coffee shop's name. "Since you didn't come down for your afternoon coffee and I needed to close the shop, I figured I'd bring it to you before I left."

Surprised, Scarlett checked the clock on one of the bookshelves. Sure enough, two o'clock had come and gone while she wasn't aware. "Time got away from me."

Allie crossed the room and gave her the cup.

"Thank you," Scarlett said. "I would have missed it quite a bit by the time the museum closed."

Allie perched on the corner of Scarlett's desk. For a woman who almost buzzed with constant energy, Allie often plunked down on Scarlett's desk, even though there were several chairs in the office that would have offered a far more comfortable seat.

Scarlett took a sip of the mocha. "Delicious as always."

Allie motioned to the roses drooping sadly in the vase on the desk. "You know you have to put water in the vase with cut flowers, right?"

Scarlett regarded the vase. As she watched, a petal fell off one of the roses. "They are in water. In fact, they were fine until they went into water. Then they immediately started to wilt. By the time I leave for the day, they'll be nothing but bent stems, and all the petals will be on my desk."

"That's horrible." Allie picked up the fallen petal, turning it over in her long fingers. "But what makes you think it's going to get worse?"

"I've gotten a weekly delivery of roses since I started here. They all do the same thing." Scarlett grabbed the florist card and handed it to Allie. "And they all come with the same card."

Dropping the petal back on the desk, Allie leaned closer to squint at the card as if that might morph the glyphs into words she could read. "Are these real hieroglyphics?"

"Yes," Scarlett said. "It says 'usurper,' and since they began when I started this job, I assume someone doesn't approve of my being here."

"That doesn't make sense," Allie insisted. "Everyone here loves you, and it's not as if you stole someone's job. Hershel Smythe was an old dear, but he told me dozens of times that he was ready for retirement."

"I never met him," Scarlett said. "Though he left me a whole binder of suggestions to help me through the transition. He was thorough, which I really appreciated."

Allie laughed. "You should have heard him order coffee. He included the exact temperature of the water and the amount of cream measured in milliliters. He was never mean about anything, but he was certainly picky."

"Maybe he's realized he doesn't enjoy retirement," Scarlett suggested.

"If that were the case, he'd go ahead and call Devon," Allie said. Her attention strayed to the wilting flowers. Several more petals had fallen, and Allie pushed them with her finger as she shook her head. "This isn't his style at all."

"Well, it has me stumped," Scarlett said. Running her hand through her thick hair, she gathered it together tightly before letting it fall to her shoulders again. It was a nervous habit, a holdover from the days when pulling her long red hair into a messy ponytail was the first step in getting down to business on a dig. "Everyone I've met since I've gotten to Crescent Harbor has been so kind and supportive of the museum. I suppose whoever it is will get bored with it eventually."

Allie frowned. "Maybe it's better if they don't."

"Why?"

"If the person is upset enough to invest that kind of money, then

I don't think boredom would stop them. It wouldn't be good if this escalates. What if the person becomes violent?"

"Oh, you're fun," Scarlett said, trying to laugh off Allie's idea.

"I'm extremely fun," Allie said with a spark of her usual sassy humor. "But I do think you need to do something about this. Does Winnie know?"

Winnie Varma was the head of security at the museum. Winnie seemed tiny compared to Scarlett who was five feet eight, especially since Winnie favored Converse sneakers. Despite her slight stature, Winnie could be surprisingly intimidating. She was intelligent, quick-witted, and often all-business. Devon had described her to Scarlett as the crime fighter and computer whiz he'd hired to protect his precious artifacts.

"I don't need to bother the head of security over some wilted flowers," Scarlett replied. "Besides, Winnie is busy preparing for the arrival of artifacts from Egypt."

Allie's eyes lit up. "I've always wanted to see a real mummy."

"It's only on loan from a museum in Cairo," Scarlett said. "As are some of the artifacts, which makes it doubly important that every piece is kept safe before, during, and after the exhibit. That means Winnie has more than enough on her plate."

"Fine," Allie said. "Don't complain to me when Winnie yells at you for not telling her about the threatening gifts."

Scarlett waved the card. "It's hieroglyphics, not a death threat."

"How's the new exhibit going?" Allie asked, changing the subject. "I heard the design was straight out of a horror movie, as befits a good mummy exhibit."

Scarlett had to admit that description wasn't wrong. Because she'd wanted to capture the eerie feeling she'd gotten once or twice when creeping through ancient crypts, the exhibit would be moody and atmospheric.

"I've raided the storage rooms as well as tagged some pieces from the collection to move to the new exhibit," Scarlett said. "I've hired a couple of local carpenters to help build the maze I envision. The basic framing was already done when last I checked, and everything was clad in plywood, which is less than spooky. But I think it'll be very effective when it's finished. I want the visitors to be in near darkness except for spotlights on the exhibits."

Allie shivered. "Straight out of a horror movie." Then she grinned. "When do I get to see it?"

"You should hold off until it's done," Scarlett advised. "That way the work in progress doesn't spoil the illusion. You'll be glad you did."

"I'll wait until Uncle Devon gets here," Allie said. "Have you heard when he's going to arrive?"

Allie had confided in Scarlett that her parents were friends with Devon before he became a tech billionaire, and they remained close. Allie considered Devon her uncle, and he'd offered her the job of running the museum's coffee shop five years before. She'd told Scarlett that she'd accepted once she saw how incredible the surfing was at nearby Luna Beach.

"Actually, I haven't heard much at all," Scarlett said. "Trying to work out the details of the exhibit through emails and rare phone calls has been frustrating. I wish he'd answer my calls—or at least return them."

"That doesn't sound like Devon." Allie sighed. "Though he has become more reclusive lately. I think he's tired of the media attention, and it's making him grumpy."

"I'm looking forward to meeting him," Scarlett said.

"You're going to love him," Allie said. "And his personal assistant is great."

"I haven't dealt with his personal assistant," Scarlett said, reaching for a pen to make a note. "What's his name?"

"Peter Vore," Allie said. "We dated years ago, and we've stayed friendly whenever Devon comes to town. Given how hard it is to be friends with an ex, I think it's a huge credit to his character."

Scarlett nodded as she jotted down his name. "Do you have his number?"

"I'm afraid not," Allie said. "I mostly call Devon directly and only chat with Peter when they're here. Devon is pretty involved with his schedule, but he says Peter is his brain."

"Maybe I can find his number," Scarlett said. "I really need some answers from Devon. I have so many questions, and time is not on my side."

"Devon always answers my calls," Allie said. "Do you want me to contact him?"

Scarlett didn't relish the idea of Allie working as some kind of go-between. It didn't sound professional to her, but she was getting a little stressed. Questions were piling up, and she needed answers before the exhibit opened. She didn't even know the exact day the mummy and artifacts were due to arrive. "Yes," she said finally. "Please call and tell him I need to know the mummy's arrival date."

Allie hopped off the edge of the desk. "No problem. I haven't talked to Devon in a couple of weeks, so it'll be nice to catch up. I'm off to the beach right now, but I promise to call when I get home."

"I don't mean to sound pushy or ungrateful, but is there a reason you can't call him sooner?" Scarlett asked.

"I don't have his number with me," Allie explained. "He made me promise not to put it in my cell phone in case I ever lost the phone."

"I see," Scarlett said, wondering if her new boss was being extremely cautious or paranoid. "Thanks. And happy surfing."

"Always." Allie practically skipped out of the office.

Scarlett couldn't help but chuckle. Having read all the personnel files, Scarlett knew Allie was two years older than Scarlett's forty years, but her friend radiated eternal youth. "Maybe I should take her up on the offer to go surfing sometime and see if it will do that for me," she muttered under her breath.

Scarlett shifted the drooping flowers to one side of her desk, causing another small avalanche of petals that she pushed away. She leaned back in her chair and thought about what Allie had said. She decided she would chat with Winnie about the flowers, but there was no hurry. She nudged the vase over another half inch, and several more petals dropped.

Her father's voice popped into her head. "The best time to deal with a problem is right now." It was a guiding principle he had imparted to his archaeology students at the university before he retired, and Scarlett had applied it many times. Why was she putting off dealing with the flowers?

"Because this new job still has me feeling off-balance," Scarlett said aloud and hated recognizing the hesitancy. She was an adventurer, not a fretter. She practically jumped out of her chair. "Time to take charge."

Since Scarlett was already standing, she considered going in search of Winnie, but she wasn't completely sure where in the museum she might be. Instead, Scarlett picked up her phone and called her. "I need to talk to you about something."

"I'm on my way," Winnie said, then ended the call before Scarlett could tell her that there was no rush.

Scarlett stared at the phone in her hand. *Now there's a response my dad would approve of.*

When Winnie arrived, she listened to Scarlett's explanation of the wilted flowers with clear annoyance. "You've had a stalker since you started three weeks ago, and this is the first I'm hearing about it? You do know I'm head of security, right? Your security falls under my job description as much if not more than the art and artifacts here."

"I don't think it's a stalker," Scarlett said. "It's some kind of weird practical joke. If I had to guess, I'd assume someone else wanted this job."

The line between Winnie's dark eyebrows smoothed, and her expression changed from annoyed to thoughtful. "I never heard of Devon considering anyone but you, but I wasn't part of the selection process. He never even asked me to do a security check on you."

"So you don't know my background?" Scarlett asked.

"I didn't say that," Winnie replied. "Once I knew Devon had chosen you, I researched you. Your qualifications were impressive, though that wasn't my main focus."

"Thanks, I think," Scarlett said. She had worried a little about her qualifications. She was an experienced archaeologist. She had a master of arts in archaeology from Cornell University in Ithaca, New York, and she'd spent years working in the field and in minor curator positions in various museums in New York City. But being the sole curator of such an impressive collection as the one held by the Reed Museum was a big step up.

"Allie mentioned the previous curator retired," Scarlett said.

Winnie nodded. "Hershel Smythe is a nice man, but he must be in his eighties. He'd seemed tired in his last months here."

"That means he definitely wasn't pushed out," Scarlett said. Allie had assured her that he wasn't, but Scarlett couldn't imagine any other reason for the flowers, and it frustrated her.

"He retired of his own free will," Winnie said. "Besides, I can't picture Hershel sending wilting flowers. The man is downright courtly." She took the card from the desk and slipped it into her pocket. "I'll track down the florist, find out who's doing this, and make it stop."

"Thanks," Scarlett said. "But don't make it a priority. I'm sure you have plenty to do for the upcoming new exhibit."

Winnie picked up the vase of flowers and grinned. "It won't be a bed of roses, but I can multitask."

Scarlett laughed. Most of the time the head of security projected a no-nonsense attitude, but Scarlett had learned that Winnie loved puns and wasn't ashamed of using them.

Winnie spun so briskly that a trail of petals followed the action.

As Scarlett watched her march out of the office, she almost felt sorry for whoever had sent the flowers. She had no doubt that Winnie would swiftly end the prank.

Scarlett settled down to go over expenditures for the upcoming exhibit. She knew the Reed Museum was fortunate not to face constant financial concerns. Since founding the museum, Devon had been more than generous with it. That helped a great deal with a large exhibit. It was expensive to move a mummy and provide a climate-controlled resting place that met the preservation requirements of something so old and fragile. She'd had inquiries from a few local colleges for a chance to study the mummy, but since Scarlett hadn't been able to get through to Devon, she didn't know how to respond.

With a sigh, she realized she couldn't complete the majority of tasks related to the exhibit until she spoke to Devon. "At least there's one thing I can do," she muttered as she got up and left her office.

Scarlett headed for the special exhibit room that would be used for the mummy. It was adjacent to the present Egyptian art and artifacts section, allowing visitors to move easily through all the Egyptian content. She stopped in the art and artifacts section to admire a lighted display of ushabti.

She'd been planning on moving all the small Egyptian funerary figures from the display along with some canopic jars to tiny lighted alcoves in the twisting maze of the new exhibit. Not all the pieces would be from the same period as the mummy, but she could note that on the identification cards. And she knew most visitors wouldn't notice.

Scarlett spun slowly, assessing the entire exhibit space. If she took all the ushabti and canopic jars, it would leave the contents of this room to the contemporary art from Egypt. That would offer visitors a contrast between the dark, winding exhibit showcasing the ancient past and this big, airy room that highlighted the fact that Egyptians were still creating amazing works of art.

Now to check out her first large addition to the museum—the Egyptian crypts. She left the brightly lit exhibit space and stepped over the velvet ropes that kept the public away from the special exhibit room when it wasn't in use.

As soon as Scarlett opened the door to the room, darkness fell over her like a shroud. She blinked and stood completely still as her eyes adjusted. When she could make out the walls of the maze in front of her, she discovered the carpenters had already applied a faux stone finish to the wooden structure they'd built. The result was perfect, reminding her of actual ancient crypts. Of course, they weren't planning to try to reproduce the smells of dusty decay and stale air that also came with ancient crypts. Visitors wanted only so much verisimilitude.

Scarlett stepped into the maze, knowing she wouldn't need to traverse much of it in the dark. She would run into the carpenters' work lights eventually. As she crept carefully through the space, she noted the rough openings cut into the maze walls where displays would appear. Right now, they simply wrecked the illusion of the stone since she could see the wooden framing in each small opening.

She stopped at one opening and peeked into it, searching for the wiring that would allow the display spaces to be lit. Then she heard shuffling footsteps. She peered ahead as far as she could, but she saw nothing.

A soft cough came from the darkness.

"Phillip?" Scarlett called, though somehow her voice wouldn't come out louder than a whisper. Clearly the eeriness of the maze had gotten to her more than she'd thought. "Max?"

Neither of the carpenters answered her call.

Then who was there? Refusing to submit to the thrill of fear along her spine, Scarlett moved away from the hole in the wall and marched deeper into the maze.

The maze only got darker until her eyes were no longer able to compensate, and she had to put out a hand to help her make the turns. *I need to tell Max and Phillip to rig up some kind of temporary lights. This is too creepy even for me.*

With a renewed stiffening of her courage, Scarlett rounded another corner only to be hit by a blinding light. "Hey!"

Almost immediately, the light dropped away from her face and toward the floor, but it wasn't soon enough to avoid dazzling her.

Scarlett stumbled forward a couple of steps and ran right into a tall man covered in dust. Her blood ran cold when she realized he held a knife.

2

With what Scarlett chose to imagine was a quiet yelp but was actually more of a shriek, she jumped away from the knife-wielding stranger. She quickly put some impressive distance between them and continued to retreat.

"Wait," the man said. "It's okay. I'm sorry for scaring you."

"Fine," Scarlett said, raising both hands. "But put down the knife."

The stranger glanced at the weapon in his hand and smiled. "It's not a knife, but I don't mind putting it down." He set the blade in the nearest display alcove, then aimed his flashlight on it.

Scarlett realized he hadn't been lying. It wasn't a knife. It was some sort of flat tool, possibly the one used to spread the faux stone finish on the plywood walls. Embarrassment over her fear became annoyance. "Who are you anyway?"

The man's smile widened.

Scarlett thought it was a nice smile. But she wasn't in the mood to be complimentary, so she scowled at him.

He held out a hand. "Luke Anderson. I'm helping Max."

"I hired someone to help Max," Scarlett said, not softening in the least. She didn't shake his hand.

A clumping came from farther inside the maze, and the man they'd mentioned appeared. Max Northrup was a bulky man in his fifties, and he filled the space as he joined them. "I see you've met Luke," he said pleasantly.

"Yes," Scarlett said tightly. "Why is he here?"

"I ran into Luke at Burial Grounds," Max explained as he rubbed the back of his neck. "Since he occasionally builds sets for the Greek to Me Playhouse, I asked if he could spare some time to help me put the finish on the walls."

Scarlett knew about the theater. Hal Baron, one of the main docents, was part of the group that performed there. In fact, Hal was the one who'd recommended Max for the handyman job.

"I agreed right away," Luke said.

Scarlett schooled her expression into something that hopefully resembled affability. "Thank you for helping out," she told Luke, making a major effort to speak calmly. Then she returned her attention to Max. "In the future, I'd appreciate it if you cleared it with me before hiring more help."

"Max didn't hire me," Luke said. "I have a job. I'm volunteering because I love this museum, and I've known Devon for years. I know everyone here, except you." He smiled again. "And now we've even rectified that."

The warmth of his smile was chipping away at her annoyance, but Scarlett wasn't quite ready to let it go. "That's kind of you," she acknowledged. "Max, do you need me to hire more people for this job?"

Max harrumphed. "No, I would have plenty of people if Phillip had shown up. As it is, I'm lucky Luke is used to rescuing people."

Scarlett wasn't sure what the last remark meant, but she assumed it was some reference to Luke's work as a set builder for the theater. She didn't see any reason to reproach Max, especially since he wasn't acting particularly repentant. Instead, she waved a hand at one of the walls. "I was admiring this stone finish. It's quite effective in the low light."

Max scratched his head with the hand that held his flashlight, making the beam swing wildly around the maze. "It's a smart bit of fakery. Luke and I came up with the finish when we were building sets for a Halloween play a few years ago."

"That was one of my favorites," Luke said, then turned to Scarlett. "Have you seen any of the plays at the Greek to Me Playhouse?"

"Not yet," Scarlett admitted, uncomfortably aware that she felt a little flushed when Luke focused his warm brown eyes on her.

"You'll have to catch the next one," Luke insisted. "Mention it to Hal, and he'll tell you all about it."

"Hal does love the theater," Max agreed.

Scarlett nodded. Hal and his wife, Greta, were the two main docents, and they'd proven to know nearly everything about the theater, the museum, Crescent Harbor, and the history of California. Scarlett always learned something every time she had a conversation with the lively couple.

Scarlett decided to focus on the immediate problem. She asked Max, "Why didn't Phillip come in today?" Phillip Bentley was a good twenty years younger than Max, and he had come highly recommended.

"I don't know," Max said. "He didn't call in. I didn't want to complain to you since I know you've been so busy, but I mentioned it to Winnie."

Scarlett figured she didn't have anything to worry about in that case. Winnie was sure to track down what had gone wrong. And Max's remark about being busy reminded her of the piles of paperwork on her desk that mostly needed information she didn't have yet. "Thank you both for the hard work you're doing. I should get to work on my own tasks."

"Sorry again for scaring you," Luke said. "Maybe I can make it up to you sometime. I could buy you a cup of Allie's amazing coffee."

She considered the offer. Was he being friendly or flirty? If it was the latter, she didn't have time for it, no matter how handsome the handyman was. A new job was more than enough to deal with at the moment, but she said something pleasant and noncommittal before leaving Luke and Max to their task.

When Scarlett reached her office door, she hesitated, still reluctant to face the papers lurking inside and the answers she didn't have. Of course, she'd known that the job of curator was mostly administrative. Someone had to keep the museum running, and much of that job involved paperwork. Normally, she didn't mind as she found it a challenge for her active mind, but right now it was her body that still hummed with restlessness and frustration.

In a bid to avoid her work a little longer, Scarlett decided to extend her walk around the museum. After all, sometimes a curator needed to make sure the people were happy too.

As she passed from room to room, she witnessed the peaceful mood of the museum working its magic on the visitors. In one of the special exhibits, a college-aged woman stood near a glass display and sketched the design from an ancient Roman coin. In another, a man leaned close to a frieze, examining the beautiful design. Though the exhibit rooms were large and often had high ceilings, the low lights provided a feeling of coziness.

When Scarlett reached the stairs, the lighting grew brighter for the safety of the patrons. The stairs were wide, and the ceiling above them was almost impossibly high. Taking a moment to admire the amazing wrought iron chandelier, Scarlett promised that she'd never grow so used to this museum that she'd forget to appreciate the incredible beauty behind every corner.

At the bottom of the curving stairs, she entered the lobby, where the tall windows at the entrance let in a lot of light. Low benches on every wall gave visitors a place to rest or congregate.

Halfway down the long room, Scarlett spotted Greta Baron leading a group of elementary school children into the ancient American gallery, and she considered following them. Scarlett enjoyed listening to Greta's tours. No one was more knowledgeable about the exhibits. While her husband's passion was theater, Greta's was history. A former history professor at Santa Catalina College, Greta always had a new and interesting fact to share on every tour, which kept people coming back again and again.

Before Scarlett could make up her mind to follow Greta, she heard her name called and turned toward the entrance doors.

Winnie waved at Scarlett. The head of security was standing next to a slender young man whose coal-black hair was an exact match to Winnie's own. However, his expression did not mirror Winnie's eternal calm. He appeared angry.

Scarlett hurried over to join them.

"I want you to meet Dr. Sayed Kamal," Winnie said to her. "Dr. Kamal, this is the curator of the Reed Museum of Art and Archaeology, Scarlett McCormick."

The man scowled at Scarlett. "I have come from Cairo to ensure the security of Usewatu as well as the priceless artifacts accompanying the mummy."

"I see." Scarlett knew the name of the mummy because Devon had mentioned it in an email. Usewatu hadn't been a pharaoh, but he was an attendant to a pharaoh, which had made him a man of some standing during his lifetime. Unfortunately, Devon had not told her that Usewatu was arriving with his very own security detail. "I'm sorry I wasn't here to greet you. I didn't realize you were coming."

Sayed waved away her apology. "Such pointless courtesies are of no consequence. I wish to know what you are doing to ensure the safe arrival of Usewatu later today."

Scarlett almost gaped at him. This was the first time she'd heard of the mummy's arrival, and it was expected today. Once again, she felt a flare of annoyance at Devon. "Was Mr. Reed aware that you would be joining us?"

"Of course," Sayed snapped. "It is the only way the mummy would be released for travel to this country. We have seen far too many priceless antiquities damaged during these ridiculous touring exhibits. It is a desecration."

"We will allow no damage to Usewatu or any of the rest of the antiquities on loan to us for this exhibit," Scarlett assured him. "Perhaps you would both come with me to my office so we can discuss the security procedures in place." *And maybe you can tell me all the other things Devon should have mentioned.*

"I suppose that would be acceptable," Sayed said. "As long as we follow up by a tour of where Usewatu will stay before and during the exhibit."

"Yes, that will be fine." Scarlett gestured in the direction of the stairs. "This way, please."

Halfway across the lobby, Winnie received a call and stopped to answer.

Scarlett waited beside the Egyptian professor who was nearly vibrating with impatience.

"We need to continue this conversation downstairs," Winnie said when she'd finished her call. "A shipment has arrived on the loading dock. I assume it contains the artifacts Dr. Kamal mentioned. I have directed that the crates be taken to a climate-controlled storeroom for opening."

"You are surprised by this?" Sayed asked.

"We weren't told the shipment's exact arrival time," Scarlett said smoothly. *Or date. Or a great many other things that would have made our lives easier.*

"Then let us go and see this room," Sayed insisted. "I wish to see that it is safe, and I will oversee the unpacking."

"It is completely safe," Winnie said crisply.

"We will oversee the unpacking together," Scarlett said. She had no intention of constantly deferring to Sayed while he was behaving so imperiously. She hadn't seen any credentials yet, but she assumed Winnie had. Her head of security was far too careful to have taken the man at his word.

The difference between the basement of the museum and the upper levels was almost startling. The ceilings were lower, and the total footprint of the basement was barely half the size of the sprawling museum above. Everything about the space was utilitarian. The air was cool and dry to keep all stored items in optimal condition. There were small workrooms and security offices and much larger storage rooms. Though the basement was clean and well-lit, the closest it came to decor were signs identifying the purposes of the rooms.

They arrived at the double doors of the largest climate-controlled storeroom to find the shipment being wheeled in on handcarts. Scarlett vaguely recognized the men maneuvering the carts. She'd met every employee when she started the job, but the ones she didn't interact with on a daily basis were harder to remember.

Scarlett scanned the room. Each of the wooden shipping crates had its own space on the cement floor. The crates were numbered, but it was easy to see only one was the right size and shape to house a mummy.

Scarlett grabbed a pry bar from a rack mounted on the wall of the room and carried it over to the long crate. "This must be Usewatu."

"You're going to open it?" Sayed asked, his voice almost dripping with horror at the idea.

"Once I am sure this crate contains the coffin holding the mummy, yes, I will open it." Scarlett examined the crate, hoping to find more shipping labels. When she'd worked at museums in the past, the documentation of shipments had been plentiful to ensure no confusion about the contents of each crate. But this shipping container was virtually bare beyond the name of the museum, a number, and cautions about fragility and the need for the crate to stay dry. "I don't suppose you helped pack these boxes in Egypt?"

Sayed drew himself up straight, offense plain on his face. "I did not. I am not a menial worker."

"Too bad. It doesn't appear that the menial workers were big on documentation." Scarlett circled the crate. It was possible that the documentation was somehow stuck to the underside of the crate, but that would be highly unusual and would suggest the crate had rested on its side at one point, judging by the arrows painted on it. "Winnie, see if you can catch the truck that delivered this. It's possible it's still at the dock. I want to know where all the paperwork went."

Winnie nodded and hurried out of the room.

Scarlett scanned the room again. The large crate simply had to house the mummy unless Cairo had sent the poor thing folded up. "We need to open this crate so we can be sure of its contents."

"No," Sayed said firmly. "Usewatu must be exposed to air as infrequently as possible."

"The entire basement is climate-controlled for best protection of the artifacts we work with here," Scarlett explained. "This room in particular is scrupulously maintained at an exact temperature and humidity." She tapped her knuckles on the crate. "I won't necessarily need to open the mummy's coffin. I'll only make certain it's inside."

Sayed stared at the box for several moments. Finally, he said, "The coffin holding Usewatu must be in there. No other crate in this room is large enough."

"To be absolutely certain, we will check," Scarlett said. "In fact, I intend to open every crate and log the contents since we are seriously lacking in proper documentation from the sending site."

Sayed stammered a bit, but he stepped away from the crate. He clearly wasn't happy, but he couldn't argue with the facts in front of them.

Scarlett slid the end of the pry bar into the crack of the crate and heaved against the lever. It took several tries before the nails in the crate gave and the lid began to lift.

Scarlett had barely shifted the lid a crack when she caught a whiff of something distinctly different from the dry, musty scent she expected from an ancient coffin or a mummy. She'd come into contact with many mummies, and she couldn't remember any of them smelling this bad. "Judging from the odor, I'm afraid some sort of vermin must have gotten into the crate and died."

"I knew it!" Sayed shouted. "Usewatu should never have left Cairo. I demand you close the crate immediately to prevent further damage and send the mummy back to Egypt as soon as possible."

"You realize that doesn't make any sense, right?" Scarlett asked as she shoved the pry bar under another bit of edge and threw her weight against it. "From the smell, the damage was done well before it got here. And I will need to see if whatever died in there has damaged the coffin housing the mummy."

With a groan, partially from the crate and partially from Scarlett, the nails finally gave completely, and the lid of the crate pulled free. Desperately hoping that she wouldn't find the mummy had been ravaged by vermin, she lifted out a layer of excelsior.

With each wad of packing material Scarlett removed, she expected to find a dead rat. She could think of no other creature that might crawl into a shipping crate as it was being packed. Instead, she merely found the ancient Egyptian coffin she'd been expecting.

The wooden coffin had the traditional shape associated with a mummy's case—a carved face at the top, then slightly broader shoulders before tapering steadily toward a narrow foot. Traces of paint showed that the carved face had originally been in full color, probably to resemble the living Usewatu.

A faded strip of hieroglyphics in white ran down the center of the coffin. Though they were fairly worn, Scarlett suspected she'd be able to translate them without issue once she had more time with the coffin. She'd taken in all these details in seconds before she noticed the most shocking thing of all.

The lid of the coffin wasn't sealed. Either from rough handling or intentional desecration, the coffin was cracked open.

"I need to open the coffin," she said. "It's not properly sealed."

Sayed pushed in beside her, gaping down at the coffin in horror. "Who would have done such a thing?"

"I don't know," Scarlett said, "but we need to find out exactly how bad it is."

"But the damage," the man protested.

"We must check," she said. "Don't worry. I know how to be careful with precious pieces of history. This isn't my first mummy."

Only the coffin did not contain a mummy. Instead, a far more contemporary man was inside the coffin. He appeared to have been poorly wrapped in the tattered remains of a torn sheet. It reminded Scarlett of a homemade Halloween mummy costume.

The man's face was uncovered. His eyes were closed, but wire-rimmed glasses still rested somewhat crookedly on his nose. His skin was inhumanly pale, making his gray hair and beard almost dark in contrast. Although Scarlett had never met this man, she'd seen many photos of him, and she had no doubt of his identity.

It was Devon Reed, and he was very, very dead.

3

With her arms wrapped around her, Scarlett huddled miserably against one wall of the climate-controlled basement storeroom. She felt chilled through and wished she could have blamed it on standing so still in the cool, dry air, but she suspected far more of the blame belonged to having found a dead man in a box.

She watched as the body of Devon Reed was carefully lifted from the mummy case to a stretcher. Though the movements were professional and efficient, competence could offer the man nothing now. Scarlett fleetingly wondered how long she'd been annoyed with a dead man for not returning her calls.

The storage room positively buzzed with activity, and Scarlett was involved with none of it. Technicians poked through any remaining excelsior in the crate and shoved handfuls of the packing material into evidence bags. Despite loud complaints from Sayed, the coffin itself had been examined, swabbed, and dusted for prints as well.

Scarlett shifted her gaze to Sayed. The man stood glaring up at Police Chief Gabriel Rodriguez. In Sayed's defense, the chief had a booming voice, and he was tall and thickly built. His mop of thick, gray hair gave him an unkempt air that Scarlett suspected sometimes led people to underestimate him. But it had taken only one look into his dark-brown eyes for her to recognize his sharp intelligence.

As Scarlett watched, Sayed answered questions with little more than grunts whenever possible. Standing beside the chief and Sayed, a young officer jotted down everything that was said. Scarlett couldn't imagine how the poor officer was translating Sayed's responses. She assumed it was similar to transcribing a chat with an annoyed bulldog.

With a sigh, Scarlett wished she could go upstairs with the other museum employees. The chief had sent Winnie to gather everyone, and an officer had tagged along to begin the questioning. Scarlett doubted that they would be able to offer any information of value to the police. Also, she knew her duties were right here as long as there were so many people milling around the crates of artifacts.

The police chief stepped away from Sayed and walked toward her.

Scarlett could feel her nerves twitch, and she reminded herself that she wasn't afraid of the police chief. She didn't actually know Rodriguez. At least, she'd never spoken with him. She had seen him in the choir at Grace Church. Until today, she'd had no idea that the big man with the beautiful singing voice was the chief of police.

I should make a list of all the things I didn't know. Scarlett had a grim suspicion this wouldn't be her last surprise of the day. Still, that didn't explain her flurry of guilty nerves. She hadn't done anything wrong. What was it about facing police officers that triggered a guilt impulse?

"Can you tell me who besides yourself handled the crate where the deceased was found?" Chief Rodriguez asked her.

Scarlett thought about it. Sayed had fussed about her opening the crate, but she couldn't remember him physically touching it. Winnie had briefly touched it when she'd run into the room at the sound of Scarlett shouting, and she'd immediately called the police. "I think Winnie may have touched it," Scarlett said. "I don't believe Sayed did. And the workmen who brought the crates into this storage room would have touched it."

"Can I have their names?" the chief asked.

"I don't know them off the top of my head," Scarlett admitted.

"There's a log, though. We record the names of everyone who handles any artifact at any point there. Winnie can show it to you. I saw a couple of men wheeling in the smaller crates after I arrived downstairs, but I didn't pay much attention to them. And it probably wouldn't have helped much if I had. I don't yet know all the staff by name."

"I'll check the log," Rodriguez said as he continued to study her through narrowed eyes.

Scarlett fought the urge to shift nervously. She wished she'd paid more attention to the workers, but she trusted the security team at the museum, and she wasn't ashamed of that. Considering she'd had no idea the crates were arriving today, she felt she'd done the best she possibly could.

"Once the crates were left in this room," Scarlett said, feeling uncomfortable in the silence, "only Winnie, Sayed, and I had anything to do with them. By the time I opened the crate, Sayed and I were the only ones in the room. I had to pry the crate open, so I'm sure none of the staff could have tampered with it between its arrival and my opening the crate. There simply wasn't time."

Past the police chief, Scarlett saw another officer, a woman with dark-brown hair pulled into a messy ponytail, walking over with a clear evidence bag. Scarlett could see it contained a piece of paper. Was this some of the documentation Scarlett hadn't found on the crate?

Responding to the drift in Scarlett's attention, Chief Rodriguez pivoted on his heels and watched the officer approach. She handed him the evidence bag. The chief looked at the paper through the bag, then held it up for Scarlett to see it. "Can you read this?"

The paper was covered with hieroglyphics. Scarlett stared at it in horror. Could Devon's death be related to the flowers she'd been getting for weeks? Should she have taken them more seriously? Could she have saved the man's life?

"Can you read this?" the chief repeated, his booming voice jerking her out of her thoughts.

Swallowing against a sudden dryness in her mouth, Scarlett translated the hieroglyphics aloud, "'All people who make evil against this tomb and destroy it, may snakes be against them on land.'"

Rodriguez flipped the page around and frowned at it. "Does that make any sense to you?"

"It's a corruption of a larger, fairly well-known curse found at the pyramids in Giza," Scarlett answered.

"Is that where the mummy that belonged in the crate came from?" the chief asked. "Giza?"

"No, he was a rather minor official, and he didn't warrant a grand tomb." Scarlett motioned toward the paper. "The original hieroglyphics of that curse say, 'All people who enter this tomb who will make evil against this tomb and destroy it, may the crocodile be against them in water and snakes against them on land. May the hippopotamus be against them in water and the scorpion against them on land.' This message is much shorter, but it's obviously based on that curse."

Rodriguez glanced at Sayed, who watched them with an almost blank expression. "Do you think the person who wrote this message was some sort of Egyptian scholar?" the chief asked.

"Maybe," Scarlett said. "But not necessarily. It's a well-known curse, and a simple online search would bring up several links to the original hieroglyphics with a translation. If it had been an original curse, that would have required actually knowing how to read hieroglyphics, so it would have suggested the writer was a scholar." She motioned to the evidence bag again. "This could be done by anyone with a computer."

"Mr. Reed could have written it himself for some reason," the chief mused. "Or perhaps someone who worked with him."

"You should check with Devon's assistant, Peter Vore," Scarlett said. "He might know who made the note or if Devon was having problems with anyone."

"Do you have any contact information for him?" Rodriguez asked.

Scarlett shook her head. "I only learned of his existence today from Allie Preston. She knows Peter and Devon personally."

"Yes, I know Miss Preston," the chief said. He didn't elaborate beyond that. Instead, he regarded the bag containing the note for a moment, then grunted softly as if he'd come to some conclusion in his head. He handed the bag to the officer who had waited patiently behind him. She hurried away with it.

"There is something you should know," Scarlett said hesitantly.

Rodriguez immediately focused on her.

The chief's intense stare nearly made her falter, but she knew she had to tell him about the previous notes. "For the last three weeks, since I began this job, I've been getting anonymous gifts of flowers with notes written in hieroglyphics."

"More curses?" he asked.

"No," she said. "They've been written on the flower shop cards. They have all said exactly the same thing: 'usurper.'"

"What does that mean?" the chief asked.

Scarlett assumed he wasn't asking for a dictionary definition. "I don't know. I thought maybe someone was upset that I'd gotten this job." She felt frustrated that she wasn't being particularly helpful. "It's been weird. Every note has come with roses that wilt and die after I put them in water, though they seem fine when they get here."

Rodriguez raised his eyebrows. "When did you last receive one of these deliveries?"

"Earlier today," Scarlett said. "Winnie has the flowers and card because she was going to look into the florist. I have the cards from the other two deliveries in my office."

The chief waved over the same female officer who'd delivered the note. "Please take Miss McCormick to her office and collect the florist cards," Rodriguez instructed. "Then pick up a third card and flowers from Miss Varma. She should be upstairs with the officers questioning staff."

"Yes sir," the officer said crisply. She gestured at Scarlett. "If you'll come with me?"

Scarlett followed the officer, wondering if the woman was as scared of the police chief as she acted. "I'm Scarlett McCormick. The chief didn't mention your name."

"Nina Garcia."

"Is the chief always so grumpy?" Scarlett whispered.

"He's not grumpy," Garcia whispered. "Mostly."

By then, they'd reached the doorway to the storage room. Scarlett was surprised to see Luke standing in the doorway.

He greeted Scarlett and Officer Garcia, then tilted his head to indicate the direction they'd come. "I see this brought out the big guns. I hope the chief hasn't been bellowing."

"That would be terrifying," Garcia agreed.

Scarlett's attention jumped from Luke to Officer Garcia in astonishment. Why was a handyman so chummy with the police? And why was he downstairs at all? He didn't qualify as staff, despite helping Max in the new exhibit, so wouldn't he have been cleared out by the police along with the rest of the museum's visitors?

To Scarlett's increasing surprise, the chief walked over and clapped Luke on the shoulder.

"I'm glad to see you," Rodriguez said to Luke. "You're not here to take over, are you?"

Take over? Scarlett was completely lost. She leaned closer to Garcia and whispered, "Why would a handyman take over?"

The officer grinned. "Luke is FBI."

FBI? Scarlett repeated silently, wondering what was going on.

Luke had clearly overheard this exchange, and he offered Scarlett one of his engaging smiles. He answered the chief with a shake of his head. "Nope, it's still your case. I came down because Scarlett's staff was worried about her. No one is telling them anything, so I volunteered to beard the lion in search of information."

"I assume I'm the lion." Rodriguez laughed, a sound that boomed as much as his voice.

"Well, it's not Officer Garcia," Luke joked.

Officer Garcia gave a shy smile.

"Information flow is buttoned up at this point in the investigation," the chief said, his voice only mildly chiding. "I can't exactly send someone upstairs with updates."

"I understand that," Luke said. "But now that I have seen Scarlett, I can assure her staff that no one has brought out the thumbscrews."

"There's no need for that," Rodriguez said. "Miss McCormick can tell them herself on the way to her office." He flapped a hand at Scarlett and Officer Garcia, clearly intending them to move along.

Since Scarlett didn't want to cause trouble for Garcia, she didn't comment. As she followed the officer, she heard the chief ask Luke if he could unofficially pick his brain.

"Of course," Luke said.

Then Scarlett and Garcia were out of range. Though Scarlett had been relieved at the idea of leaving that cold storage room, now she longed to go back. The mystery of the volunteer handyman who just happened to be FBI had piqued her interest.

"Can we stop by wherever my staff is?" Scarlett asked. "The chief said I could show them I'm all right."

"Sure," Garcia said. "I have to ask Winnie about the flowers anyway.

But please don't say anything about the investigation. The chief was serious about information flow. He'd have my head."

"We wouldn't want that," Scarlett said supportively.

As they walked, Scarlett was distinctly aware of the sound of her heels against the cement floor of the basement. The ringing sound echoed, increasing the isolated feel of the basement. Scarlett had been in museum basements dozens of times, since that was often the location of the workrooms assigned to junior staff. She'd never found them creepy or scary, but she'd never found a dead body in a crate before either.

"Did you know Devon Reed?" Scarlett asked.

"No, I don't know any billionaires," Officer Garcia replied. "What did you think of him?"

"I never actually met him," Scarlett admitted. "I talked to him on the phone a few times. He was always kind and warm, maybe a little eccentric. I was excited to meet him."

The officer winced. "I'm sorry it had to be like this."

Yeah, death was no way to make an acquaintance. Ever.

4

When Scarlett and Officer Garcia reached the first-floor lobby where the museum staff waited in small groups, it felt as if everyone focused on Scarlett at once. She could practically feel the weight of that much attention.

Hal and Greta hurried toward Scarlett and Garcia, and Winnie was at their heels.

"I'm so glad you're all right," Greta said, grabbing Scarlett's hands. "We knew someone died, but no one would tell us anything." She aimed a reproachful frown at Winnie.

The head of security merely shrugged.

"Greta was worried it was you," Hal said to Scarlett.

Greta gave her husband a sharp look.

"All right, *we* were worried it was you," Hal amended. "No one remembered seeing you for a while. Luke promised to see what was happening. Did he find you?"

"He did," Scarlett said, "and I'm fine."

"Then who died?" Hal asked.

Scarlett felt Officer Garcia's warning hand on her arm, but she'd already known better than to answer the question.

"All your questions will be answered in due time," the officer said. "Now Miss McCormick and I need to go to her office." She faced Winnie. "Will you accompany us?"

Winnie acted mildly surprised by the request, but she quickly agreed.

They left the barely mollified group in the lobby and headed upstairs to Scarlett's office. Along the way, Garcia explained that the police chief wanted her to collect the wilted flowers and the florist card that Scarlett had given Winnie.

"The flowers are in the security office in the basement," Winnie said. "I can hand them over to the techs in the storage room, or you can come down with me after you're done with Scarlett."

The officer appeared to consider it for a moment. "I'm assuming you've already handled them."

Winnie nodded.

"So have I," Scarlett added.

"Then it's probably fine for you to go ahead and get them," Garcia said. "Someone in the storage room will direct you where to put them. Do you need an evidence bag?"

Winnie shook her head. "I have plenty." She spun on her heels and strode toward the stairs that would take her to the basement.

Scarlett realized that she'd never even seen the security office. Winnie came to her whenever called. Of course, the museum was large and Scarlett probably couldn't be expected to know every nook and cranny in a few short weeks, but she still felt guilty.

"Are you all right?" the officer asked her.

Scarlett noticed she'd slowed down considerably as she'd been thinking. "Sorry. I'm fine." She picked up her pace again, and they soon arrived at her office.

"It's okay not to be fine," Garcia remarked as she followed Scarlett into the office. "You did discover a dead person."

"Yes, I remember." Scarlett saw the officer wince and felt guilty again. She was normally good with people, but she felt off-balance. Maybe she wasn't *quite* fine.

"This is a lovely office," Garcia said.

Scarlett stopped and scanned the large room. She hadn't made much of a mark on it yet, but it was lovely. The desk was a gorgeous mahogany with hand-carved trim, and the chairs were all padded in buttery leather. The floor-to-ceiling bookshelves had been partially filled with books when Scarlett took over. That had been a surprise, but Scarlett assumed that the retiring curator simply hadn't needed books on ancient antiquities or management anymore.

"The office hasn't changed much from when I arrived," Scarlett admitted. Then she crossed the rest of the way to the desk and opened a drawer. She retrieved the florist cards and held them out to the officer.

Garcia opened an evidence envelope. "You can drop them in."

Scarlett did as instructed.

As the officer sealed the envelope, she glanced around the room and exclaimed, "What a beautiful cat." She gestured toward a photo of Scarlett's fluffy black cat, which rested on one of the bookshelves.

"Thank you," Scarlett said. "That's Cleo."

"As in Cleopatra?"

Scarlett nodded.

"How appropriate." Garcia smiled as she walked over to peer at the photo more closely.

Scarlett was glad to see the officer didn't reach out to pick up the photo. The silver frame tarnished quickly with handling.

"Is she big?" Garcia asked.

"Yes, she is," Scarlett replied. "She's not a purebred cat, but I suspect she may have some Maine coon in her gene pool. And she can be a shedding machine. Still, I can't imagine life without her."

"I wish I had a cat," the officer said wistfully. "In fact, I'd probably have several, but I have such a crazy work schedule. Does Cleo miss you terribly when you're gone?"

"Not too much," Scarlett said. "She's independent, but she's also sweet. I'm not above bringing her to work, cat hair and all." Then she had a thought. "Can I ask you something?"

Garcia blinked. "You can ask, but I can't promise I'll be able to answer."

Scarlett acknowledged her response with a nod. "It's Allie Preston. Her family and Devon Reed were close. Allie thought of him as an uncle. She's going to be devastated. Can I call and tell her about Devon's death? She shouldn't hear it through the grapevine."

"Let me ask." Garcia called the chief and explained what Scarlett had told her. "From what I have heard about Devon Reed, Allie Preston may be as close as we will come to local next of kin. I want to go to her house and let her know about the man's death. And I'd prefer to take Miss McCormick with me."

Scarlett held her breath for the moment of silence after Garcia's request.

Finally, the chief agreed to the idea. He directed Garcia to drop off the florist cards with a tech before leaving the building.

Scarlett felt a sense of relief, but she dreaded breaking the tragic news to Allie. How would her friend cope with the terrible loss?

Allie's tiny bungalow was about a block from the beach, so Scarlett assumed it was the best place to check for her friend unless she was still out surfing. The blue Craftsman-style house had a porch on the front. When Scarlett noticed Allie's surfboard propped against one of the columns of the porch, she was certain she'd made the right choice. This was reinforced by Allie's red Jeep Wrangler parked in the short driveway.

"She's home," Officer Garcia said as they pulled parallel to the curb. "I thought we might have to walk down the beach to Allie's favorite surfing spot."

"You know where Allie's favorite surfing spot is?" Scarlett asked.

Garcia laughed. "You have surely noticed what a determined surfing evangelist Allie is. Hasn't she managed to drag you out yet?"

"She's tried, but I've had my hands full since I moved here." Scarlett opened her door, but before stepping out, she asked, "Do you surf?"

"No, I discovered I'm happier when my days off are a little less death-defying."

When they reached the house, the officer knocked, then moved back, putting Scarlett closer to the door.

Allie swung it open and beamed at them. "What a pleasant surprise. I didn't realize you two knew each other."

"We only met today," Scarlett said. "At the museum."

Allie's cheerful expression slipped away to be replaced by puzzlement. "What can I do for you both?"

"We need to tell you something," Scarlett said. "It's about Devon Reed."

Allie took a step away from the door as her expression morphed into fear. "I tried to call him right after I got home from the beach. I thought maybe he wasn't getting phone reception. Sometimes he goes to places that are off the beaten track."

"I'm very sorry to tell you that Devon Reed is dead," Garcia said, her voice gentle. "His body is at the museum."

Allie gaped at her, the color draining from her cheeks. "At the museum?" she echoed faintly. "Did he have a heart attack or something? He never mentioned being ill, so I assumed he was in good health."

"I found him," Scarlett said. She suspected she wasn't supposed to reveal any details, but she didn't care. There was no doubt that Allie had loved this man. She'd considered him family. She deserved the truth. "He was left in the Egyptian coffin where the mummy should have been."

Allie leaned her head against the door, clearly processing this new and horrifying information. "But why? Why would anyone do that?"

"That's what I hoped you could help us with," Garcia said. "Can you think of any enemies Mr. Reed might have had? Had he mentioned any recent difficulties?"

"I haven't actually spoken to him in a couple of weeks," Allie said weakly. "Do you mind if we sit down? I'm feeling a little wobbly."

"Of course," the officer said.

They walked into the house and settled on chairs in Allie's bright living room. The theme of the room was nautical with lots of white and a few wicker accessories. All in all, it was the least appropriate place Scarlett could imagine to discuss a possible murder.

"Devon and I would often go weeks without chatting," Allie said. "He was so busy, and sometimes he traveled to parts of the world where phone calls were much harder to make." She shuddered. "If he was in a mummy case, does that mean he died in Egypt?"

"Maybe," Garcia said. "We aren't sure of much at this point. Did he tell you about any sort of problems he had been having?"

"Last time I talked to Devon, he didn't mention any trouble, but he never did," Allie said. "I think he always saw me as a little girl, so he wouldn't have said anything to upset me." Her voice cracked. "I should drive to Petaluma and be with my parents. They knew Devon for many years before he became successful. Dad says Devon was a nerdy dreamer who imagined technology no one else believed in."

"Are you okay to drive that far?" Scarlett asked.

"I think so," Allie replied. "I won't make it to work tomorrow. Mom is going to want me to stay."

"Don't worry about the coffee shop," Scarlett said as she rested her hand on Allie's arm. "Family is more important."

Allie hugged Scarlett and finally began to cry. She asked nearly incoherent questions for which neither Scarlett nor Garcia had answers.

5

As it happened, there was no reason for Scarlett to find a replacement for Allie to run the coffee shop since the museum was closed Thursday at the rather strong request of the police. Scarlett didn't try to fight it. Everyone needed some time to deal with the loss of Devon Reed, especially since so many of the staff had known him personally.

Of course, closing the museum didn't give everyone the day off. Scarlett didn't feel right about staying home, though she'd called Max Northrup to halt work on the special exhibit maze for a few days. She'd phoned Phillip Bentley as well, but the call had gone straight to voice mail, so she'd left a message.

Scarlett knew she'd have to make a decision about the new exhibit. Even though the mummy was missing, it was possible she could make it work with the other artifacts and the mummy's case. But it was all up in the air until she knew more.

When Scarlett had called Winnie, the head of security insisted that she and her staff would be there on high alert. "We don't know enough to be certain the museum isn't under threat."

Scarlett couldn't argue. In fact, worries about the museum and everyone connected with it had kept her awake most of the night.

She still had a lingering headache as she walked into the museum at her usual time Thursday morning. When she entered the lobby, Hal and Greta rushed over to her. For a sleep-deprived moment, Scarlett wondered if she'd failed to let them know the museum was closed.

Hal handed her a tall cup of coffee.

Scarlett was surprised to see the words *Burial Grounds* printed on the side of the cup.

"I have keys to the coffee shop, and I thought you'd probably need a cup," Hal explained. "I even called Allie to ask how you take your coffee."

"Thank you," Scarlett said. As she inhaled the enticing aroma, she was flooded with appreciation for the kind gesture. "How is Allie?"

"She's being brave," Hal said. "Her main concern was how we're all doing."

"We've been worried about you," Greta said, taking Scarlett's hand. "Witnessing what you did and then being questioned by the police."

"I'm fine," Scarlett said. "You didn't need to come in today, though I am grateful beyond words for the coffee." She took a sip and found it as delicious as ever. Perhaps it would ease her headache as well.

"I tried to tell Allie and Greta that you were probably fine," Hal said, putting his arm around his wife. "But when Greta fusses like a mother hen, I might as well be speaking to the sea."

"Oh, hush," Greta told him, then leaned closer to Scarlett. "He was worried too. Don't let him fool you."

"I'm touched," Scarlett said. She studied the couple's matching expressions of concern and realized she'd come to consider them as much a fixture of the museum as the exhibits themselves. They'd become essential to her so quickly. Everyone in the museum had.

She was especially touched by their concern, considering their loss had to be much sharper than her own. "I expect you've had the harder time. I assume you both knew Devon Reed."

Greta nodded. "Hal and I met him at a fundraiser for Santa Catalina College. I was a history professor, and Hal was a theater professor, so we were expected to charm donors as best we could."

"We can be quite charming," Hal said with a grin that wiped years from his age.

"One of us can anyway," Greta said, giving him a gentle poke with her elbow. "But I don't think either of us could compare with Devon. He was charismatic and gracious. And he gave the college a rather large endowment."

"When he founded this museum, he asked us to consider becoming docents," Hal said. "We enthusiastically agreed. It's one of the best decisions we've ever made."

"You considered Devon Reed a friend?" Scarlett asked.

"Oh yes," Greta said. "Though we haven't seen much of him lately. He has become rather reclusive, and his visits to Crescent Harbor have been few."

"It surprised everyone here because Devon loved this museum," Hal said. "Whenever he was in town, he'd spend whole days and half the night wandering the museum. I'd sneak away whenever possible to walk with him. He had a fascinating story for every object. Some of my best material as a docent came from those visits."

"I'm sorry I never got to know him," Scarlett said before taking another sip of coffee.

"That was a surprise too," Greta said, curiosity sparkling in her eyes behind dark-rimmed glasses. "No one expected Devon to hire a new curator without meeting in person. When he hired Hershel Smythe, Devon spent weeks here to acquaint Hershel with every tiny thing about all the artifacts and pieces of art."

"That would have been nice," Scarlett said. "I do feel a bit like I was thrown in the deep end. I'd hoped Devon's first visit would give me time to hear more about the collection directly from him, since he assembled most of it."

"I'm sure he would have," Hal said loyally. "As much as Devon grew a bit more distant over the years, the one thing I know is that nothing would have made him lose his love of this museum."

Scarlett smiled, hoping that was enough since she didn't have anything to offer about the man they clearly cared for. To Scarlett, he was a disembodied voice and the author of dozens of emails. "I do appreciate you both coming in, but you don't need to stay. At this point, I don't know when we're reopening. Or if we're reopening at all."

"Are you sure you don't want me to remain on coffee duty for the staff?" Hal asked.

Scarlett chuckled. "I'm sure they would be happier if you did, but it's up to you."

"We'll stick around a little longer," Hal said.

"I do have one other question," Scarlett said. "Did either of you ever meet Devon's assistant, Peter Vore?"

"Yes," Greta said. "Peter always traveled with Devon. He's extremely competent and friendly in a slightly shy way. Devon once said Peter's job was to be his left brain because Devon's head was always in the clouds."

"He must know something is wrong," Scarlett said. "At the very least, he must think Devon disappeared."

Hal and Greta exchanged glances.

"That *is* likely," Hal said. "I'm sure the police will find Peter and ask him."

"I'm sure you're right." Scarlett raised the cup. "Thank you both again."

The couple waved and started toward Burial Grounds.

Scarlett headed to her office, where she spent an hour trying to sort out which things she needed to deal with immediately and which were out of her hands until the police were done with the museum. Her hopes for Hal's coffee chasing away her headache quickly fell through. If anything, it only made her feel more on edge.

She was certain that explained the way she practically launched from her chair when someone pounded on her office door. The door flew open before Scarlett could even round her desk.

Dr. Sayed Kamal marched in. "What are you doing to locate the remains of Usewatu?"

"Good morning to you too," Scarlett said, refusing to let the man's accusatory tone upset her. "I'm afraid that is a police matter since the mummy was removed from the mummy case, probably for the purpose of putting the dead body of Devon Reed in his place."

Sayed clutched his head dramatically, making Scarlett wonder if the man was purposefully putting on a show. "This is everything as I feared. I warned time and again that lending the mummy to a spoiled, rich American would result in horrible desecration."

"And the death of the American you insulted," she said dryly.

"Of course," he acknowledged before collapsing on a leather chair not far from the door. "But it is my job and my heart to guard the antiquities of Egypt, so my sympathies lie with the mummy. Who knows what kind of conditions Usewatu is experiencing?"

Since Scarlett didn't see the value of that line of questioning, she asked, "When did you last see the actual mummy? Did you travel to the United States on the same ship?"

"No, I did not," Sayed said. "I flew. I had some last-minute business in Cairo, so I could not leave when the ship sailed. But I did oversee the packing of all the artifacts."

She jumped on his admission. "You must have seen the original shipping documents. I assume they were in order then."

"Yes, but it was not my job to keep up with the paperwork beyond that," he replied testily. "My job was the security of the items, and I know that Usewatu was safely in the crate when the ship sailed. I would stake my reputation on it."

"Too bad you couldn't travel with them," Scarlett said, though mostly she found it suspicious.

"I wanted the mummy and the artifacts sent by air," Sayed growled.

"It is much safer. Airports have more security, but sometimes museums are mired in the past." He shrugged. "And in poor budgets."

"You believe sending by ship was a money-saving choice?" She found that surprising. Surely Devon could afford to pay for whatever travel was best suited to keeping the collection safe.

"I believe so," he said, his tone disapproving. "It is true that Devon Reed paid handsomely to acquire the mummy, even temporarily, for this museum. But I think some people felt economizing on the transport would put more of the money in their own pockets."

"Is that common?" Scarlett asked.

"Is greed not common all over the world?"

She found the theory unlikely. If Devon had wanted the mummy sent via air, she had no doubt he would have made it happen. It was apparent he had been actively involved in the transit. Otherwise, how would he have ended up inside the mummy's coffin?

"Was Mr. Reed intending to travel with the mummy on the ship?" Scarlett asked.

Sayed snorted. "I have no idea what that American planned. His travel arrangements were hardly of concern to me. What is being done to find the mummy?"

"Since you say you are certain the mummy was in the crate when it was loaded on the ship, it means that the mummy was removed from there. I know the police will be searching the ship. They may find the mummy today."

"They had better locate Usewatu." He leaped to his feet and pointed at her. "And he had better be in perfect shape."

At Sayed's threatening tone, Scarlett felt an icy chill. He was clearly passionate about the protection of the artifacts, but she knew passion and obsession were not far apart. Both could lead to violence.

How far had Sayed's passions driven him?

6

For the rest of the morning after Sayed's angry outburst, Scarlett worked at her desk with her office door open, feeling somehow claustrophobic at the thought of being shut away.

When she finally sat up to stretch her stiff back, she realized she hadn't accomplished much beyond catching up on her more mundane paperwork. It wasn't that she lacked more pressing things to do, but there were so many loose ends that she had no way to tie up.

Scarlett decided to list the things someone else had to do before she could act. She needed the police to release the storage room so she could finally check all the artifacts. She needed them to release the mummy's coffin so she could decide if it would be enough draw to continue with the exhibit. A man had died for that exhibit. Did that mean she owed it to him to finish it, or should she shut it down out of decency?

With a groan, Scarlett wrote down Devon's name. He was the primary benefactor for the museum. No one else even came close, and the previous curator had made little or no effort to secure additional funding outside the money Devon continuously donated. She needed to make some plans for fundraising, but it was possible she should wait on that as well. The museum would almost certainly be in the billionaire's will. Was it disrespectful to even think about money the day after the man's body had been found?

She leaned forward and rested her head in her hands, letting her hair fall forward to make a red curtain around her face. It was surprisingly comforting, shutting out all the questions that had no answers.

Scarlett was still sitting in that position when she heard a rap on the doorframe. She sat up fast, alarmed at the idea that Sayed had returned to berate her some more.

Thankfully, the woman in the doorway holding a cup of coffee and a manila folder was both familiar and friendly. Winnie walked in and gestured toward Scarlett's hair with the folder. "Some days I think about taking my hair down and doing a little hiding too."

Scarlett realized she'd never actually never seen Winnie's hair down. The head of security always wore it in a tight ponytail. Scarlett had pulled her hair up frequently when she worked on archaeological digs, but her wild red mane was never as smooth and orderly as Winnie's.

Winnie held up the cup of coffee. This one didn't have the Burial Grounds label. Instead, it sported a smiling coffee bean.

"You went to Boardwalk Beans Coffee Company?" Scarlett asked.

"I didn't, but I sent out for coffee after Hal and Greta left," Winnie said as she handed over the cup. "I thought it would perk up the remaining staff."

Scarlett grinned. "Between you and Hal, I may survive this day after all." She didn't even bother to remove the lid and peer inside. She merely took a long drink of the coffee.

"Do you have a minute?" Winnie asked.

"Of course," Scarlett said, then savored another sip of the rich coffee.

"You know more about hieroglyphics than I do, and I need an expert opinion." Winnie set the folder on Scarlett's desk and opened it.

Scarlett scanned the contents of the folder. She was surprised to see the florist card she had given Winnie along with a scanned copy of the note left with Devon. "Where did you get these?"

"You gave me the florist card," Winnie replied. "Since the police took the two other cards, I convinced them that they could spare this one. And Chief Rodriguez sent me that scan after I suggested I have contacts that he doesn't." She tapped the folder. "I've been studying them. Do you think these two sets of hieroglyphics were written by the same person?"

Scarlett examined the card and the paper. Since the word *usurper* didn't appear in the longer note, she had no easy direct comparison, but that didn't matter. With the two side by side, it was obvious they were radically different. Not only were they written differently, but the style of the hieroglyphics was different as well.

"No, it's definitely not the same person," Scarlett said, feeling mildly embarrassed that she hadn't realized it with her first glance at the longer note left with the body. "This note is a shortened quote from a curse from a pyramid in Giza, but the hieroglyphics used to write *usurper* are from a different time period."

"That's strange," Winnie commented.

Scarlett examined the two samples again. "If the person is simply doing a Web search on hieroglyphics and copying the ones that say what they want, it's not surprising that the periods don't match."

"But you're certain they weren't written by the same person?" Winnie asked.

"The style of the writing itself is different," Scarlett said. "The word *usurper* is written in a heavy hand and slanted, which the original hieroglyphic the person copied wouldn't have." She pointed at specific lines. "The longer quote is written in a lighter hand, and each hieroglyphic is upright as it should be."

"Are you saying the second one could have been written by someone who knows more about hieroglyphics?" Winnie asked.

"Not necessarily. The person may simply be a more careful copyist." Scarlett waved a hand at both. "I can say that they weren't copied from hieroglyphics made during the actual time Usewatu lived. Those would not have been on or around his tomb."

A tap at the door drew their attention.

Officer Garcia peeked into the room. "I hope I'm not interrupting your work. Chief Rodriguez asked me to come by."

Scarlett rose and waved the officer in. "You're not interrupting. Winnie and I were discussing the hieroglyphics on the curse left with Devon's body. I hadn't had a chance to compare them to the ones on the florist card. They weren't written by the same person."

"Oh?" Garcia stepped beside Winnie and pulled a notepad from her pocket and began writing in tight, cramped letters as Scarlett explained what she'd told Winnie. When Scarlett finished, the officer's eyes widened in alarm. "Mummy curses sound so ominous."

"The whole idea of Egyptian curses has been overblown by movies and legends to make them sound far more exciting than they actually were," Scarlett said.

"Really?" Garcia asked. "I'll admit that I know nothing about them."

"Don't feel bad," Winnie offered. "I didn't know anything about them either, and I've worked in the museum for years. All I know about hieroglyphics is that they're little pictures."

"Stylized little pictures," Scarlett clarified. "But reading them isn't as easy as guessing what the picture represents and then automatically knowing the message. Many of the hieroglyphics were more about sound than actual meaning."

Scarlett slid the scanned copy toward them and continued her explanation. "Part of the difficulty in reading hieroglyphics lies in the lack of rules or the loose adherence to them. They are written in rows or columns. They can be read from left to right or from right to left."

The officer leaned forward and squinted at the paper. "Then how can anyone know what they mean?"

"There are clues." Scarlett pointed to a specific hieroglyph. "For instance, see this bird figure? All animal or human figures in hieroglyphics will face toward the beginning of the line, which shows me which direction the reading must be done."

"All of that to put a curse on someone." Garcia shook her head and jotted down more notes.

"Most hieroglyphics archaeologists find in tombs have nothing to do with curses," Scarlett said. "In fact, most tombs don't contain any curses at all."

"Really?" This time it was Winnie who voiced the surprise. "I thought they usually did it to scare off tomb raiders."

Scarlett shrugged. "They weren't so easily deterred. At any rate, curses *are* rare, and they tend to be direct cause and effect, almost legal in their wording. If you do this bad thing, you'll be punished in this way."

The officer shuddered. "The punishments creep me out. I remember seeing an old black-and-white movie when I was a kid. It had a shuffling mummy and a scary guy droning out a curse."

"I saw that movie," Scarlett said. "But real Egyptian curses are often less impressive. Hieroglyphics on one tomb warn that anyone doing harm to the tomb will be miserable. Another says he'll be seized by the neck like a goose. And then there's this one." She motioned to the paper. "The original warned that doing evil would make crocodiles, snakes, hippos, and scorpions be against the evildoer, though whoever copied from that message only left in the snakes."

"I suppose no one in California is going to run into crocodiles or hippos unless they work at the zoo," Garcia said. "I have seen scorpions, and I'd rather not have them against me."

"I agree," Winnie said.

The officer retreated a step from the desk. "We're trying to create a timeline for the shipment to find where the mummy was switched out for Devon Reed," she announced, taking on a slightly more formal tone. "The chief hopes to know by the end of the day."

"Have you determined the cause of death?" Winnie asked.

"There were no wounds," Garcia said. "The coroner says it was likely poison that killed him, but we don't know what kind. Tests have ruled out a number of toxins, but they haven't found the actual cause yet."

Winnie gestured toward the paper and its curse. "Could toxins include snake bite toxins?"

"The coroner said there were no snake bites on the body," Garcia replied. "The chief asked that one specifically after Scarlett translated the curse."

"Have you been able to locate Peter Vore?" Scarlett asked. "I imagine Devon's assistant would be invaluable in helping to trace the man's movements."

"We haven't found him yet," the officer said. "We haven't made nearly as much headway as we'd like. Part of the problem with exchanging information with Egyptian authorities is the time difference. Cairo is nine hours ahead of us."

Scarlett nodded. "I understand. When you do track down Peter, I'd love to speak to him. Also, can you tell me when I'll be able to gain access to the storage rooms again? Those artifacts are extremely valuable, and I need to finish logging them in."

"You should have access tomorrow," the officer assured her.

"Excellent," Scarlett said. "I need to make some decisions about the special exhibit they're connected to, which I can't do until I know the contents of all the crates. And Sayed has been extremely anxious about virtually everything related to this."

Winnie's attention visibly sharpened when Scarlett mentioned Sayed. "You've heard from him today?"

"He came by," Scarlett answered.

"How did he manage that?" Winnie asked. "The museum is closed, and access to anyone other than the police should have come through me. I would never have allowed the man to wander around the building."

"He didn't mention how he got in," Scarlett said, realizing that she should have asked. She should have recognized how odd it was that he'd simply appeared at her office door, but he'd immediately put her on the defensive. She must have been more exhausted than she thought. "I don't even know if he's left the building."

"If you'll excuse me," Winnie said, rushing to the door, "I need to find out."

As soon as Winnie left the room, Scarlett asked the police officer, "Is there anything else I can help you with?"

"Not from my task sheet, but I want to hear more about this visit from Dr. Kamal." Garcia opened her notepad again. "I know the chief will be interested."

Scarlett recounted the obnoxious man's visit. Once more, she chided herself that she hadn't asked about his presence in the museum at the time. She needed to focus.

When she'd finished with her story, Officer Garcia thanked her and left.

Scarlett settled into her chair and sipped her coffee, grateful to discover it hadn't gone completely cold. She cast one fretful glance at the door before booting up her computer. If she couldn't work on the exhibit, maybe she could work on finding a few answers.

She began her search with the name *Dr. Sayed Kamal.*

The rest of Scarlett's workday had proven both uneventful and a bit frustrating. Dr. Sayed Kamal was easy enough to track to the museum in Cairo, where he was clearly a minor functionary, despite the airs he'd put on every time he'd spoken to Scarlett. She'd been glad to know Sayed was the person he claimed, but she hadn't come any closer to figuring out what to do next.

When she finally gave up and went home, she was grateful for the sight of her cozy white Mission Revival house. It was only one story, which Scarlett appreciated. It made the whole building feel snug and efficient, and Scarlett loved efficiency. She also approved of the bright, airy rooms with their exposed beams. She'd filled the house with plants, carefully chosen to be safe around her cat, Cleo.

When Scarlett opened the arched front door, she immediately heard Cleo meowing in noisy greeting. Scarlett slipped inside quickly, closing the door behind her. She dropped her bag and scooped up the fluffy black cat. "I missed you."

Cleo butted Scarlett's chin with her head, which Scarlett took as a return of the sentiment.

"Give me a second, and we'll have a long cuddle," Scarlett promised the cat. She carried Cleo through the kitchen and dining area and out onto the deck.

The deck had an unusually high railing that had been nearly turned into a wall by the strategic addition of heavy screening to discourage Cleo from climbing over it and dashing off in search of trouble. Eventually, when Cleo was more settled in her surroundings, Scarlett intended to remove the screening so the view would be less obscured.

Scarlett kept several flowering plants and small trees in pots on the deck, and they needed frequent watering even in September. She knew some of them would have to be brought in soon because the weather was growing distinctly cooler. She set Cleo down, and the cat twined through her legs as Scarlett watered the plants.

"It's such a beautiful day," she said as she finished. "How about you and I have dinner out here tonight?"

Cleo meowed.

"I'm glad you agree." Scarlett carried the cat inside, but she didn't lock the door since they'd be going back out shortly.

She walked through the kitchen, pausing only long enough to peek into the fridge. She didn't feel like starting dinner yet, so she decided to sit down for a few minutes. She deserved a rest after such a long day.

Scarlett carried Cleo to the sectional across from the fireplace in the large open living area. She emptied her pockets onto the round table in front of the sofa and settled down, curling her legs under her.

Cleo purred contentedly while Scarlett recounted her day. If the cat found the story of the obnoxious Sayed disturbing, she showed no sign.

Scarlett idly picked a fluff of black fur from the white upholstery of the sectional and wondered exactly why she was so drawn to white furniture when she had a black shedding machine in the house.

Cleo nudged Scarlett's hand, protesting too long a pause in her petting.

Scarlett rubbed under Cleo's chin. "I know being the curator of such a fantastic collection is a dream job. But these last two days have been more of a nightmare. Speaking of which, I definitely need more sleep tonight. I'm thinking warm milk before bed."

Cleo didn't respond. She'd fallen asleep.

"Now you're showing off," Scarlett murmured, settling deeper into the comfortable upholstery. She gazed up at the round mirror over the fireplace. It reflected the long space behind her, which included the kitchen. She considered what to prepare for dinner, but before she could make a firm decision, her eyes drifted shut of their own accord.

Hours passed while Scarlett dreamed of wandering the empty halls of the museum, searching for the mummy of Usewatu. She kept catching glimpses of movement from the corner of her eye and hearing a soft shushing sound as if from someone shuffling along in rough socks.

Scarlett was sure the sound came from the mummy lumbering around the shadowy corners, but no matter how hard she tried to catch up, the mummy managed to stay out of direct sight.

"Wait!" Scarlett called out in the dream. "I need to put you in your coffin!" She raced around a corner—only to find herself face-to-face with the mummy.

Usewatu knocked her down, then leaned over and sunk impossibly sharp fingernails into Scarlett's thigh.

With a shriek, Scarlett jerked awake to discover that it was Cleo, not an ancient Egyptian mummy, who'd sunk claws into her leg. Mildly disoriented, Scarlett surveyed the living room and realized it had grown dark while she'd slept. "Oh," she said softly to Cleo. "I think we missed dinner."

Cleo sunk claws into Scarlett's leg again, not deep enough to draw blood but enough to smart.

"Hey!" Scarlett cried.

A crash sounded behind her.

Scarlett came abruptly and completely alert. She spun on the sofa fast enough to see movement in the kitchen.

It was an intruder.

7

In barely restrained panic at the realization of an intruder in her home, Scarlett lunged for the table where she'd emptied her pockets, scrambling for her phone. She tried to keep a hand on Cleo, but the cat slipped free and jumped to the floor. Scarlett watched the kitchen through the mirror above the fireplace in case the intruder decided to rush her.

With her back arched and her fur puffed out, Cleo yowled at the top of her lungs.

Scarlett realized the cat had dashed into the kitchen. "Cleo!" she shouted, rage pushing aside panic at the idea that her pet could be hurt by the intruder. "Don't you dare touch my cat!" She climbed over the sectional to get to the kitchen quicker, not caring about the white upholstery.

Cleo yowled again, and someone thumped into the dining table. The intruder was moving farther away.

"Cleo!" Scarlett shouted as she ran for the dining room.

One of the glass doors thudded as it was flung wide open.

When Scarlett reached the kitchen, she flipped on the light without pausing, hoping to illuminate the intruder. But the dining room was empty. The only sign of life in the room was Cleo. The brave cat stood in the doorway to the deck, her tail flicking furiously.

Scarlett scooped up the cat before Cleo could take it upon herself to pursue the intruder outside. Together they walked out onto the deck so Scarlett could close the deck gate that hung open.

At the gate, Cleo gazed out at the moonlit yard.

"Did you scare away the bad man?" Scarlett asked Cleo softly.

Cleo finally stopped glaring into the darkness long enough to nudge Scarlett's chin with the top of her head.

"My hero." Scarlett secured the gate and walked back inside. She shut the back door firmly before dialing the police.

Fridays were normally busy at the museum, but once Scarlett dodged the crowd of reporters outside, the halls of the museum were empty. Scarlett understood that the police didn't want patrons in as long as the basement was a crime scene, but the silent museum was disquieting.

The door to Burial Grounds was open, and she spotted Allie in the lighted space beyond. Scarlett walked in. "I thought you were going to stay with your parents for a few days."

Allie gave her a pale imitation of her usual effervescent smile, then began fixing Scarlett a cup of coffee. "I considered it, but my folks didn't need me. We exchanged some stories about Devon, but they seemed fine leaning on each other. Besides, I need to be here with my stuff and my work, right in the thick of things. I've never been a stay-on-the-fringes kind of person."

"That I can believe," Scarlett said. "Still, I'm impressed you braved the crowd of reporters outside. I thought the shouting and camera flashes were overwhelming."

"I suppose they're doing their jobs." Allie handed Scarlett her cup of coffee. "Devon was important to Crescent Harbor. The reporters are trying to give people the information they want."

"That's generous of you." Scarlett sipped the coffee gratefully as she studied her friend. Allie wore a subdued air of sadness that Scarlett had never seen on her. Though Scarlett had hardly known Devon, Allie's grief made the man's death real for her, which made no sense. Surely seeing the dead man would have made it real. *But emotions are what they are*, she thought.

Allie leaned forward to examine Scarlett's face. "You're a little pinched around the eyes. Are you okay?"

"I'm fine. Now." Scarlett sighed. "Last evening someone broke into my house."

Allie gasped. "What?"

"Well, not broke in exactly," Scarlett amended. "I'm pretty sure I left the door unlocked and then fell asleep on the couch with Cleo. When I woke up, we had an intruder."

"That's horrible," Allie said. "Are you all right?"

"I'm fine," Scarlett answered. "I never got near him. I think Cleo chased him out of the house before he could steal anything. Because the house was dark at eight thirty in the evening, the police figure that some burglar thought no one was home."

"Wouldn't a burglar have been suspicious about the open door?" Allie asked.

"You'd think." Scarlett suppressed another sigh. "I guess he and I both made a mistake last night."

"It sounds terrifying," Allie said. "I leave my doors unlocked way too often. I don't expect break-ins around here."

"As the police were quick to remind me, break-ins can happen anywhere." Scarlett idly drummed her fingers on the plastic lid of her cup, recalling the conversation with the police officer. It had been embarrassing to be scolded that way, but she deserved it. "The prevailing theory is that I must have woken up right after the guy came in. Otherwise, he wouldn't have been in the kitchen. Apparently, kitchens are not the wealth center of most homes."

"It's possible it wasn't even a burglar," Allie said. "Maybe it was one of those reporters, searching for a scoop. After all, if the guy was scared of a cat, he doesn't sound like a professional criminal."

Scarlett considered the idea. On one hand, she hoped reporters wouldn't start showing up at her house. On the other, a reporter was probably not going to kill her and Cleo in their sleep.

"Can I get some coffee?"

At the sound of the familiar voice, Scarlett and Allie turned toward the coffee shop doorway.

Winnie surveyed both of them. "You two look as exhausted as I feel."

"I don't know what you're talking about," Allie said in a decent facsimile of her usual breezy tone. "I'm bright as a bunny."

"Winnie, I have a question," Scarlett said, intent on changing the subject before Winnie could ask anything about her own appearance. She didn't want another scolding about unlocked doors, so if she could keep Winnie in the dark about the break-in, she would. "Did you ever find out how Sayed got into the museum yesterday?"

Winnie crossed the room and leaned on the counter. "No, and I asked everyone, though one of my new hires acted incredibly suspicious, avoiding eye contact and such. I suspect he didn't want to fess up to that kind of security breach, so I'll keep an eye on the guy and be sure he's learned his lesson."

"You sound pretty sure," Scarlett said. "Considering it's based on a hunch."

"I'm a good judge of character," Winnie said. "Besides, nothing else makes sense. The man can't pass through walls. And he is associated with the new exhibit, so it's not totally incompetent that security let him pass."

"If you led with that last part, I expect you'd have gotten a confession quicker," Allie said as she handed a cup of coffee to Winnie.

"Personally, I feel sorry for the poor security guy, making a mistake like that when you're his boss. I probably would be hesitant to admit it too. You *are* scary."

"Excuse me?" someone asked.

This time all three women reacted, pivoting almost as one to see a stranger in the doorway. It was a young woman in her twenties with a head of dark curls.

The woman peered at them through wire-framed glasses. "Can you point me toward the curator?" she asked, her voice hitching up in a way that was both hesitant and questioning.

"I'm Scarlett McCormick," she said, walking toward the woman. "I'm curator of the Reed Museum of Art and Archaeology." Scarlett wasn't quite sure why she'd introduced herself in such a formal way, but the weirdness of the last couple of days was making her lean on formalities, probably as a form of comfort in the familiar.

Winnie hurried around Scarlett and reached the woman first. "Please tell me who you are and how you got into the museum."

The young woman stared at Winnie in alarm. "I'm Beatrix Morrow," she squeaked. "I told the man at the door that I'm Devon Reed's assistant, and he let me in. I haven't been able to reach Devon by phone." She tilted her head to see Scarlett. "I was hoping you could help me find him."

Allie rounded the counter and made a beeline for the stranger. "You are not Devon Reed's assistant," she snapped. "Devon's assistant is a man named Peter Vore. I've known him for years."

Beatrix took a step back through the coffee shop doorway, visibly frightened by Allie's unusually hostile tone. She cleared her throat. "Peter Vore was the last assistant, and I'm the current one." She raised her chin. "My boss will tell you. Is he here? I know his ship docked in Redwood City the day before yesterday."

"You were Uncle Devon's assistant, but you weren't traveling with him?" Allie demanded.

Beatrix stiffened slightly. "I was following his instructions," she said, her voice becoming firmer. "I arrived yesterday as planned, but I discovered Devon had never checked into the hotel. That's not like him at all. He can be a little eccentric, but he's extremely punctual." She regarded Allie for a moment. "Since you called him Uncle Devon, may I assume he's staying with you?"

Allie's face fell.

Scarlett spoke up so Allie didn't have to break the tragic news. "I'm sorry to tell you, but Devon isn't here. He died."

Beatrix's knees buckled, and it was only because Winnie was so close to her that the woman didn't hit the floor. Winnie caught her by the arm, holding her up.

Scarlett closed the last few feet between them and grasped Beatrix's other arm. "Come and sit down."

"I think I'd better," Beatrix said.

Scarlett and Winnie helped the woman to one of the benches outside the coffee shop. By the time Beatrix was seated, she'd begun to sob.

Allie had trailed them at a distance, her expression unreadable.

Scarlett sat on the bench beside the sobbing woman, fearful that it wasn't calming to have all of them looming over her. "Miss Morrow, can we get you anything?"

After a few hitches of breath, the woman removed her glasses to dab at her eyes with the edge of a finger. "Please call me Beatrix. Devon sometimes called me Bea, but I usually go by Beatrix."

Scarlett studied the young woman. She noticed that Beatrix had a scar over one eyebrow that gave her an eternally quizzical look.

"I'm so confused," Beatrix said. "Devon was healthy."

"Without a doubt," Allie said firmly.

"The police believe Devon was killed," Scarlett said.

"Killed?" Beatrix repeated. "Do you mean murdered?" The last word was spoken in a near shriek.

Scarlett worried that the young woman was going to become completely hysterical. "Is there anyone I can call for you?"

Beatrix shook her head, sending her dark curls bouncing. "I'm alone." She blinked a few times, then turned to Allie. "You were right. I should have been with Devon, but I get terribly seasick. He told me he wouldn't need me and that I should fly. He was so understanding." The last word broke on another sob.

"He was always kind and understanding," Allie agreed, her tone finally softening, but only slightly.

Winnie had been quiet all this time, but she'd stayed on her feet, watching Beatrix intently. "Miss Morrow," Winnie said, ignoring the woman's invitation to call her by her first name, "I expect the police will want to speak with you."

Beatrix widened her damp eyes. "Really? Oh, of course they would. I'm going to have so much to do." She swung her attention to Scarlett. "He sailed with the artifacts to protect them. Does this mean they were stolen?"

"I don't know for certain," Scarlett said. "The mummy was definitely missing, but the mummy's coffin is here in the museum. And there are other crates that I haven't been able to open yet. Do you happen to have a list of the items that were shipped?"

"Yes, I do, but it's at the hotel," Beatrix answered. "Do you want me to get it?"

"It would help," Scarlett said.

"We should make copies of it," Winnie said. "The police will want a copy as well."

"Miss Morrow." This time it was Allie who ignored the woman's name preference. "Do you know why Peter was replaced? He'd been with Devon for years, and I know they were close."

"Oh, I couldn't say," Beatrix said, though something in her voice suggested she probably could say a great deal on the subject.

"Do you have contact information for Peter Vore?" Winnie asked.

Once again, Beatrix shook her head hard enough to make her curls swing. "I didn't need his information. It was a clean break." She shifted on the seat. "Actually, I think he called Devon a few times. I heard them arguing on the phone. But I didn't have to talk to Peter."

"How long have you held this job?" Winnie asked.

"Not long," Beatrix said. "Only a few months. But they've been wonderful. Devon is the nicest boss I ever had."

The remark seemed to soften Allie even more. Scarlett saw the distrust wash from her friend's expression. However, Winnie still eyed the newcomer with obvious skepticism.

"Do you need help getting to your hotel?" Scarlett asked Beatrix. "Or perhaps I can get you a ride to the police station. I'm sure they'll be eager to speak to you."

"Oh no," Beatrix said. "I'll stay here if this is where the artifacts are. I know Devon would want me to watch over them."

Scarlett frowned. *Great. Another stranger who's obsessed with the artifacts.* She made an effort to speak pleasantly. "I will appreciate any assistance you can provide, but we need that list of artifacts, and you said it was at the hotel."

"Oh, right," Beatrix said.

They were interrupted by the ringing of Scarlett's cell. She pulled it from her pocket and read the screen. "It's the police. Maybe this is the notice that the storage room has been released, and we can finally check on the artifacts."

"That would be good," Winnie murmured.

Scarlett answered the call and put it on speaker so Winnie could hear as well.

Unfortunately, the call had nothing to do with releasing the storage room. Instead, the officer informed Scarlett that they had found the place where Devon Reed's body had entered the mummy's coffin.

"It's in one of the storage bays of a ship at the port in Redwood City," the officer reported. "The chief would appreciate it if you and your head of security could come down to the port. There's a problem."

"What kind of problem?" Scarlett asked in alarm. *Don't we have enough problems already?*

"The chief didn't say," the officer replied. "But he'd appreciate it if you came as quickly as you can. Can I tell the chief that you're on your way?"

Winnie glanced at Beatrix before nodding to Scarlett.

"We should be there in a couple of hours," Scarlett informed the officer. As Redwood City was part of the sprawling San Francisco Bay area, the drive would take a while.

The officer passed along the specific details of where to find the ship, but he wouldn't answer any of Scarlett's other questions.

Ultimately, the call ended with no one satisfied and worry on every face around her.

8

Although Beatrix announced her intention to go along with them to the port, Winnie put a quick end to that. She asked a member of her staff to accompany Beatrix to her hotel room so she could retrieve the list of the artifacts in the collection.

When Winnie suggested that she drive, as she knew the port area around Redwood City, Scarlett readily agreed. She was content to sit in Winnie's green Nissan Leaf and simply watch the scenery pass by her window.

The highway ran parallel to the coast for a while, and Scarlett savored the occasional peeks at the ocean. Each time she breathed in the briny scent, it reminded her of oceans and seas she'd seen all over the world. Each had its own personality. Today, the Pacific lived up to its name, appearing far more tranquil than Scarlett felt. The road also offered stretches of farmland, patches of trees, and even mysterious industrial machinery whose purpose Scarlett could only guess at.

"Do you drive this way a lot?" she asked Winnie.

"Not often," Winnie said. "Sometimes on museum business. Every once in a while, I get the urge to visit San Francisco. It's a wonderful city."

Once they entered the port, the scent of the ocean became heavier and mixed with other, less pleasant smells. The bustle of port traffic made Scarlett glad she wasn't driving. She was experienced at finding her way in unfamiliar places, but she didn't need the stress right now.

When they finally parked, nothing about the area was picturesque anymore. The port was all business, and the business was shipping goods. They found the huge, rusting ship the officer on the phone had described, and Scarlett was relieved to spot a familiar face, one of the officers she'd seen at the museum.

The officer was short and stocky with a shaved head and blue eyes. Scarlett guessed he was in his late forties. He had a calm, efficient air that she appreciated. She didn't know his name, but she strode up to him and introduced herself.

"I know who you are," he said. "I'm James Young. The chief said to show you right in."

"Good to see you," Winnie said to him. "How's your family?"

The police officer's face lit up. "They're well. Colleen's trying to talk me into a vacation."

"To see the Mayan ruins?" Winnie asked. "Or maybe Greece?"

He shook his head. "New York City. That's why it's still under discussion."

"What does Mason think?" Winnie asked.

"That kid is ready to go anywhere," Young said with a grin.

Winnie included Scarlett in the conversation by explaining, "Officer Young is a frequent visitor to the museum. He loves archaeology and ancient civilizations."

Scarlett gave him a warm smile. "Come by my office at the museum sometime, and I'll tell you stories about dig sites."

"I'd enjoy that," the officer said, then gestured toward a gangplank. "This way."

When they reached the hold where Chief Rodriguez waited, Scarlett was surprised to find Dr. Sayed Kamal there with him. She acknowledged the man with a slight nod.

"Dr. Kamal was doing his own tracking of the shipment," the chief said, his tone thick with disapproval. "He has managed to contaminate my crime scene, so he is presently in custody."

"I make no apology," Sayed snapped, raising his chin defiantly. "My concern is the mummy."

"I see," Scarlett said, drawing the words out long enough to suggest she really didn't. "But I'm not sure why you asked us to come."

"For one," the chief said to Scarlett and Winnie, "I want to know if you can verify this man's identity. I'm having trouble with bureaucratic red tape, and it doesn't help that my primary crime scene is so far outside my jurisdiction."

"I haven't found anything to suggest he isn't who he says he is," Winnie replied.

Scarlett was impressed by how noncommittal Winnie sounded. It was obvious that Winnie didn't trust Sayed any more than Scarlett did.

"I know Dr. Sayed Kamal exists and is connected to Egyptian antiquities," Winnie continued. "But I can't find any photographs of the man to confirm that this is him. With the time zone difference, I'm having difficulties finding anyone who can describe him to me. But I have calls out, and I'm waiting to hear a response."

"What are you saying?" the Egyptian howled. "Of course I am Dr. Sayed Kamal."

"Fine," Rodriguez grumbled, waving a hand. "Book him for interfering with a police investigation. I might think of some more things later."

Sayed was still making a ruckus when Officer Young escorted him out.

Winnie excused herself to make a phone call.

"I understand you wanted Winnie here to verify Sayed's identity," Scarlett said as she folded her arms over her chest. "But why did you ask me?"

"I have something to show you." The chief hurried through the hold, dodging crates.

Scarlett trotted after him until they rounded a final stack of crates to an empty space in the crowded hold. A crime scene technician in white coveralls knelt beside something on the floor. It was a single scrap of what appeared to be ancient linen.

"Was that on the mummy?" the chief asked.

Scarlett dropped to her knees to examine the scrap.

The tech scooted away to give her room.

Scarlett knew ancient linen would be incredibly fragile, and she was limited in her ability to run any tests in the hold of a ship without her equipment at the museum. She leaned close and sniffed. There was no hint of decay, but she hadn't expected any. Instead, the strip gave off a slight mustiness, exactly as it should. "May I touch it?"

"Is it necessary?" Rodriguez asked.

"It'll help," Scarlett said.

The chief agreed.

Scarlett gently lifted the scrap and inspected it as best she could under the available conditions. The linen was brown and stiff, but it wasn't completely inflexible, though the ends were fraying and flaking. The weave was loose enough that she could see the threads even in the poor light of the hold.

With the scrap still in her hand, Scarlett gave her opinion. "I see nothing to suggest it didn't come from the mummy, but I can't be truly certain without more light and better equipment."

"We have that at the police lab," the chief said.

Scarlett winced. "Please understand that this linen is incredibly fragile, and it will crumble under much handling."

Rodriguez seemed to mull it over for a few moments. "Normally, I would hand it over to you because you have much more experience with mummies than anyone in the lab, but you're connected to the case."

"I had no reason to harm Devon Reed," Scarlett said. "I never actually met him, and I felt nothing but gratitude toward him for my job. Also, I doubt this piece will survive the station's lab tests."

The chief was silent for another moment. "We found three scraps. We'll take two with us to preserve chain of custody. You take that one and do your tests. Report your findings to me immediately."

Scarlett hated the thought of leaving any scraps in the hands of the police. She had her own reverence for these tangible pieces of ancient history, but she suspected this compromise was the best she would get, so she explained to the tech how to protect the fabric.

To his credit, the tech listened attentively with the occasional question. He evidently took the care of the piece seriously.

Somewhat reassured, Scarlett requested equipment to secure and transport the fabric that would go back to the museum with her.

Once she felt confident the scraps of linen were safe, Scarlett rose, ignoring the soft creak of her joints. Clearly it had been a while since she'd squatted at a dig. She walked over to the chief. He had been directing his people from a spot where he could keep an eye on Scarlett.

"Can you tell me when I can have access to the scene at the museum?" Scarlett asked Rodriguez. "I will soon receive a list of the contents of all those crates, and I need to open them and make sure the contents are intact and complete."

"You're welcome to the room," the chief said. "We've found enough evidence here to suggest this is our primary crime scene. The hold is filthy, but that gave us footprints and signs of a struggle."

Scarlett shuddered as she scanned the dimly lit hold. What a horrible place for anyone to spend his last moments. Of course, she'd had close calls in her own career in some fairly tight spots, none of which were very clean. "I appreciate the chance to do my job. Did your team learn anything from the crates in our storage room?"

"Only the mummy crate showed signs of having been opened and rescaled," Rodriguez said. "We opened a few crates, but we found just packing material and what I assume are artifacts. I saw no reason to open them all and risk bad press for the police if anything was damaged by us. I assume the untouched crates contained valuable items."

"They should," Scarlett agreed.

"I'd prefer someone in law enforcement to be there when you first open them."

"That would be fine," Scarlett said, "as long as I can start the task today."

The chief surveyed the hold grimly, but he agreed. "I'll get someone. You can open the crates today and let me know if you find anything you didn't expect. After that, you can reopen the museum whenever you wish. There's nothing else we can do there."

With a huge sigh of relief, Scarlett went searching for Winnie. She wanted to return to the museum right away.

The drive back to Crescent Harbor felt somehow longer and more rambling, though Scarlett knew it was just her eagerness to get to work on the potential mummy wrapping and check the contents of the crates.

"What do you think about Sayed?" Winnie asked, marking one of the first things she'd said since they'd begun the return drive.

"He's passionate about his work," Scarlett said. "But I think he's going to continue making things more difficult."

"Do you think he's the real Dr. Kamal?"

Scarlett shrugged. "Maybe? I will be happy to leave that verification to you. I'd be more interested to know which person was Devon's real assistant: Peter Vore or Beatrix Morrow."

"That should be easy enough to sort out," Winnie said. "I'll get on it as soon as we arrive at the museum."

"Good, because my afternoon is going to be spent uncrating artifacts and testing linens." Scarlett remembered something. "Did you hear the chief say we could open the museum?"

Winnie pressed her lips together. "If it were up to me, I'd wait until at least Monday. I want to know for sure that everyone is exactly who they claim to be."

Scarlett could see the wisdom of that, though she hated to keep the museum closed on Saturday since it was the most common day families came to the museum together. She loved to watch parents passing on a love for art and history to their children. However, missing one Saturday probably wouldn't be the end of the world, and Scarlett trusted Winnie's instincts when it came to security.

"I'm going to think about it a little longer," Scarlett said. "But I imagine you're probably right. For now, let's say we reopen Monday." Even as she said the words, part of her wanted to vacillate, which was so unlike her that Scarlett felt a lurch in her stomach. *Relax. Finding a dead man in a box would knock anyone unsteady. Wouldn't it?*

They parted company when they entered the museum. Scarlett headed straight to the basement and the workrooms. She was anxious to inspect the mummy wrappings, not only to give the chief's promised officer time to arrive but also because she wanted to get the task over with.

Thanks to Devon's generosity and commitment to the museum, the workroom's array of equipment for any kind of artifact examination was extensive. Simply gazing around the workroom always gave Scarlett a thrill. She'd often worked with makeshift equipment due to budget constraints. "It's enough to warm an archaeologist's heart," she said aloud as she carefully carried the packaged linen to one of the workroom tables.

She carefully clipped the smallest piece from the frayed end of the linen for testing. She began one test before moving on to the next, preparing a tiny scrap for the mass spectrometer. This analysis would measure the mass-to-charge ratio of the molecules in the sample, hence the word *mass* in the machine's title. The molecular weight would reveal the chemical properties of everything present in the scrap and produce a spectrum, a plotted visual representation of the various components.

The door to the workroom opened as Scarlett was loading the sample. She finished the procedure before switching her focus. She expected to see Winnie, coming to report an update or new catastrophe. But the person waiting patiently in the doorway wasn't anyone she would have guessed. It was Luke.

"Do you mind an interruption?" he asked. "Chief Rodriguez asked me to come by to help with the uncrating of the artifacts that traveled with Devon."

"The FBI takes orders from local police now?" she asked, nonchalantly shifting her attention to flip the switch on the mass spectrometer.

"No, but I'm happy to help out, especially on this case," he replied. "May I come in?"

Scarlett wasn't sure how she felt about the arrival of the handsome agent. She remained a little embarrassed at her assumption that Luke was only a handyman, though he'd done nothing to make her think otherwise when they'd met. And his presence now didn't feel any more normal. Still, she agreed to accept whoever the chief sent. "Of course."

"You don't have to sound so excited," Luke said. "I bring news."

"I would love to hear it," she responded. "If you don't mind my working while you talk. I need to secure the rest of this sample safely. It's been through a lot already."

"Go right ahead," he said, showing no sign of being bothered by her rather cold shoulder. "The coroner says Devon was in a scuffle before he died, though he wasn't seriously injured. The coroner also discovered what sort of poison ultimately killed him. It was a venomous snake indigenous to Egypt, not Crescent Harbor."

Scarlett stopped and stared at him. "Crescent Harbor has snakes?"

"Not in abundance, but nature does find a way," Luke replied. "The coroner reports no bite marks, but he said if the bite corresponds with one of the minor injuries from the scuffle, it may have hidden it. I believe they're in the process of making a closer examination with that possibility in mind. I'll let you know if they find anything."

"How could a snake get on a cargo ship?" Scarlett asked. Though she supposed that was a silly question. As Luke had said, nature found a way, and cargo ships were commonly full of all sorts of spiders and hordes of rats, so why not a snake or two?

"There were no snakes on the official cargo list," he said. "But sometimes exotic animals travel without making it to the ship's manifest. A deadly snake wouldn't be at the top of my exotic pet list, but I understand there is a trade in them."

Smuggled snakes wouldn't explain the note on Devon's body, but she could imagine someone taking advantage of a terrible accident. "If Devon was bitten by a smuggled snake, the culprit may have wanted attention on a mummy's curse instead of searching for smuggled cargo."

"If so, it isn't working," Luke said. "Several different agencies are all over that ship now. If there were smuggled snakes aboard, even if they've been removed, some sign should remain. Last I heard, sniffer dogs had joined the search."

"You're well-informed," Scarlett said. "Is this an FBI case now?"

"Not officially," he said. "Normally, we focus on crimes that pose major threats to American society. But we can be invited in when local law enforcement finds their limited resources taxed."

She raised her eyebrows. "Is that what's happening?"

"The local police are extremely competent," Luke said, "but the chief is smart, and he knows they don't have the laboratory resources of the FBI. Plus, Crescent Harbor doesn't encounter a lot of billionaires being murdered. Devon Reed was a big deal, and his death is drawing attention."

Scarlett thought of the reporters milling around the museum. "I've noticed. My whole staff basically had to sneak in this morning to avoid the press." She related her encounter with an intruder the previous night and Allie's theory that the intruder may have been a nosy reporter.

"I hadn't heard about that," he said. His tone suggested he wasn't happy about it either. "I don't like the idea of anyone breaking into your home. I assume you live alone."

"I do not live alone," Scarlett said loftily. She refused to let Luke's clear concern work on her nerves after Allie's theory had helped calm them down. Why did she feel like she needed to talk to him in the first place?

"Oh?" Luke's expression was almost overly casual.

"I have an attack cat."

The corner of Luke's mouth twitched, but he didn't laugh. "That must be a comfort."

"Look," she said, tired of the conversation and itching to do something. "I need to leave these machines running for a while. Once they're through, the results will come to the computer here."

"What exactly are you doing?" he asked.

"I'm authenticating the bit of linen from the mummy," Scarlett replied. "With this mass spectrometry and chromatography equipment, I can detect and identify different chemicals in fragments weighing as little as a tenth of a milligram."

"Impressive," Luke said. "What would you expect to find if the linen is from the mummy?"

"Some of the materials consistent with mummy wrappings are sugar gum, oils, and beeswax." She explained the process took time, but the computer would send an alert to her phone when the tests were done. "In the meanwhile, I need to open some crates."

"Lead on," he said. "And let me help if I can."

"I've opened a lot of crates during my career," Scarlett commented as she led the way to the storage room. "But I suppose I don't mind an extra pair of hands."

Luke laughed. "Has anyone ever told you that you have a welcoming demeanor?"

The joke surprised her, and she didn't know how to respond, so she simply kept walking. Apparently, he was determined not to take offense at her standoffishness. She knew part of her issue with Luke was a slight territorial instinct she'd already developed over the museum, but part of the problem was that she didn't really know him. He'd simply landed in her life without much warning.

Then Scarlett thought of the trust everyone around her placed in Luke. *I guess if they trust him, I should too. Or at least give him the benefit of the doubt.*

With these thoughts distracting her, she grabbed a pry bar from the rack near the door and shoved the edge of the bar into one of the larger crates. Opening this crate was far easier than opening the one holding Devon's body, and the lid came up smoothly.

Finally, something easy. Scarlett reached inside the crate to move the excelsior, but she felt something firm and smooth. The object flexed, and she jerked her hand back. What could Devon have acquired for the museum that would move so easily? It certainly wasn't an ancient vase or sculpture.

"What is it?" Luke asked.

"Nothing," she said briskly as she moved the packing material around.

To her shock, something shifted inside the crate moments before the contents were revealed. A large, round chiseled block lay in the crate. But the block wasn't what had moved. Something big rested on top of the block.

It was a coiled snake. And it lunged right at her.

9

"**S**nake!" Scarlett shrieked. While watching the snake, she jumped away and bumped into Luke, then shifted around him and scrambled farther back.

The snake missed her and hit the floor of the storage room. For a moment, it didn't move.

Scarlett had a fleeting hope that it had died in the fall, but even as the thought passed through her head, she knew it was ridiculous. The snake had fallen only a few feet.

Sure enough, the snake recovered from the shock and began gliding slowly toward Scarlett.

She backed into a second pile of crates and yelped again. She was too afraid to take her eyes off the snake, so she felt behind her for the edge of the pile of crates.

"Hold still," Luke instructed.

"Tell him that," Scarlett snapped, edging sideways to get away from the snake.

She hadn't been watching Luke since her full attention was on the snake slithering toward her, but now she saw Luke step into her field of vision. He brought a pry bar down on the snake's head with a dull *thwack*. It stopped moving.

To Scarlett's horror, Luke picked the creature up. He was careful to grasp it behind the head, but that didn't make her feel much better. What if he had simply knocked it out?

Luke examined the snake. "It reminds me of a rattlesnake with the color and the patterns on its back, but these spots aren't really shaped like diamonds. I don't recognize this kind of snake." His gaze settled on Scarlett. "I assume you've traveled extensively for your job. Have you ever seen one of these?"

Scarlett stood up straight and did her best to present a calm demeanor, despite the fact that her heart continued to pound. "Snake identification is not my field, but I do try to research all the local snakes wherever I work. I have no idea when I'll encounter one, and it's best to know which ones are venomous. I believe that is an Egyptian carpet viper. They're relatively common in the areas I've visited."

"I suspect it's quite venomous." He returned to rotating the snake carefully as he examined it.

"Yes," she said. The struggle to keep her voice calm was getting harder as she watched Luke holding the snake. "They account for a great many fatalities. There is an effective antivenom, but I've also heard the bite is extremely painful." *And I nearly got to find out personally.*

"I wonder if this is the snake that supplied the venom to kill Devon."

"Supplied?" Scarlett repeated. "You think that's the snake that bit him? If so, how did it get into a different crate?"

"I haven't come up with a theory about that crating beyond the possibility of a smuggler," he said. "But I think we should open other crates and see if there are more snakes."

Scarlett did not think that was a good idea at all. In fact, her pressing desire to see the artifacts in the crates had waned a bit in light of the viper. She knew she should finish the job, but at the moment, it was the last thing she wanted to do.

Luke gestured with the snake, something Scarlett would prefer he not do. "Devon was probably not bitten. Despite the coroner's theory that a bite could have been hidden in one of Devon's cuts or scrapes, I would consider that improbable in the extreme. There are other ways for snake venom to get into a man's veins."

"That would mean Devon was definitely murdered."

He raised his eyebrows. "Did you doubt that?"

"I suppose I harbored a hope that he was bitten accidentally, and someone was trying to hide him," Scarlett said. She expected the FBI agent to laugh at the idea.

"That would make sense if he'd opened a crate to check on an artifact and was bitten by a snake someone was smuggling," Luke said, taking her idea seriously. "Still, I think someone milked a snake for venom, maybe even this one." He raised the viper. "Then the person injected Devon."

"It would make me feel better if you stopped waving that thing around," she said.

His expression registered surprise. "Oh, right. Sorry." He surveyed the room. "I need to take the snake with me so its species can be verified and we can test it against the toxin in Devon's blood. Do you have something to put it in?"

"Hold on." Scarlett left the room, making a concerted effort not to sprint for the door. Leaving the storeroom felt like the best idea she'd had all day. She walked to the workroom, pulled a large, clear plastic bag from a dispenser, and took it to Luke.

"That'll be perfect," he said, clearly delighted. "Exactly what I needed."

"We're well-supplied." She held the bag out.

"Actually, can you hold it open so I can put the snake in?"

Scarlett swallowed. *It's dead. Stop being foolish.* She'd never been particularly afraid of snakes in the wild. Of course, none of the snakes she'd encountered prior to this one had ever lunged at her. Scarlett held the bag open and fought to keep the fear off her face.

Luke slipped the snake inside and took the bag. "You did great," he said, making it plain her effort to appear brave had failed miserably.

When he carried the snake toward the door, Scarlett assumed he'd leave with it. After all, it could be a murder weapon. But he simply set the bag down near the door before rejoining her.

"You're staying?" she asked.

Luke smiled. "Don't sound so disappointed. I didn't realize you found my company so taxing."

"It's not *your* company I have a problem with," Scarlett said as she glanced at the snake.

His smile didn't waver. "You are aware that the snake is dead, right? It'll sit quietly over there in the bag. I'm not leaving until we're certain the museum exhibition wasn't being used to smuggle snakes. That's a risk you're not taking alone." He picked up the pry bar from where he'd set it after killing the snake. "I'll open the crates first, if you're okay with that."

"It's fine with me," she said, feeling a sense of relief.

"First, I should call the chief," Luke said. "He may want to send someone to retrieve the snake." He removed his phone from his pocket and walked away.

As much as Scarlett had no desire to begin opening crates on her own, she was slightly irritated at the wait. She leaned close to one of the crates and thumped on it with her knuckles, straining her ears for any sounds of movement inside. She didn't hear anything, but did that mean there was nothing inside? She wasn't sure, and that didn't help her nerves.

She was still rapping and listening when Luke approached her. "The chief is sending an officer over to pick up the snake," he said. "But we have the go-ahead to open the rest of the crates. Where should we begin?"

Scarlett pointed at the crate that had made no sound when she thumped on it. "Might as well start here."

Luke opened crates, and Scarlett carefully examined and logged the contents. They found no other snakes, though Scarlett did find a large beetle inside one of the urns. She was quite proud of herself for not dropping the urn when the beetle tumbled out. In fact, she quickly caught it.

"We can't let any insects go," Scarlett explained as she studied the beetle she held. "If this were a pregnant female beetle, she could be the first stage in an invasive species doing serious damage to the ecology." She carried the beetle to the workroom and dropped it into a small terrarium that she'd purchased for this exact use.

Luke followed her. "It's nice that you're not afraid of bugs."

"Beetles haven't killed anyone I know lately," she replied dryly.

"Good point."

Although Scarlett had done a much better job of covering it, she'd been more than a little unnerved when the beetle had appeared, proving she was far from her usual calm. Still, she appreciated that Luke hadn't commented on her obvious edginess.

If there had been any doubt, Scarlett made her anxiety perfectly clear when they walked into the storeroom and saw a person crouched down. Scarlett yelped and jumped, once again smacking into Luke. Then she felt the wash of embarrassment as she recognized two people in the room, one now standing with the snake bag in her hand. It was Officer Nina Garcia, and Winnie stood not far from her, her arms crossed.

"Sorry I scared you," Garcia said. "I came to get the snake."

"A potentially venomous snake I hadn't heard about," Winnie said pointedly.

"It's not nearly as dangerous now," Luke said.

Winnie glared at him. "As the head of museum security, I need to know when a dangerous snake is found in the museum," she said firmly. "I believe it is something that would fall under my job description."

"You're right," Scarlett said. "I was so caught up in the artifacts that I wouldn't have told anyone until the job was done. It was Luke who called the police."

"Which was the right thing to do," Garcia threw in.

Everyone frowned at the officer.

Garcia simply held up the bag. "I'll take this away." She started to leave, then stopped as if something else had occurred to her. "I should probably tell you that we had to release Dr. Kamal. We couldn't find anything on him."

"Thank you for letting me know," Scarlett said. She didn't look forward to more interactions with Sayed.

"One more thing," Garcia said. "The chief asked me to collect the mummy wrapping if you're done with it."

"I'm not," Scarlett said. "I'll see that it gets to the police station as soon as I am."

The officer glanced at Luke, and he nodded. "Okay, that sounds fine," Garcia said. "I should get to the station."

A wave of annoyance swept over Scarlett that the officer had checked with Luke. She didn't appreciate having someone else being in charge of her work.

"Have you heard any updates on the break-in at Scarlett's house?" Luke asked the officer.

Garcia blinked. "The chief thinks it was opportunistic. Apparently, the door wasn't locked."

"I would like to see the scene," Luke told her.

Scarlett was taken aback. Luke was nice enough, but she wasn't sure she wanted him in her home. She found his interest rather confusing. She figured his presence here had to do with his fondness for the museum, but why would an FBI agent care about a break-in at her house?

"I'm not worried about the burglary at the moment," Scarlett said evenly. "There are much more serious matters at hand. Thank you for your concern."

Luke's tight-lipped expression signaled his displeasure at her reply, but he didn't push it.

After Officer Garcia left with the snake, Winnie asked if she could stay for the rest of the unpacking. "In case you discover anything else deadly."

"We found a beetle," Luke said cheerily.

"Was it poisonous?" Winnie asked.

"There are no poisonous beetles," Scarlett said. "At least, not the way you mean. Some beetles secrete poison to keep other creatures from eating them, but those beetles don't attack people."

"You know beetles?" Luke asked.

Scarlett shrugged. "I once dated a coleopterist, and some facts stuck in my head."

"I assume a coleopterist studies poisonous bugs," Winnie said.

"Not exactly," Scarlett explained. "Coleopterology is a branch of entomology that specializes in beetles."

"Knowing you is going to be a constant learning experience," Luke remarked.

Scarlett studied him, not sure if he was making fun of her. His expression was admiring, which made her feel a little flushed. She quickly brushed past him and headed toward the crates. "We'd best finish up with these."

As Scarlett assessed and logged each item, she was struck by what an extraordinary collection Devon had sent. In fact, she began to wonder if they could be a little *too* extraordinary. How had Devon gotten so many incredible pieces? The value of this collection would be staggering, and the museum already had some fine Egyptian antiquities.

"What?" Luke asked.

Scarlett started as his question interrupted her thoughts. "Excuse me?"

"You seem to be bothered by something," he said.

"I'm wondering how I'm going to know which of these items are on loan from Egypt and which are now part of the museum's permanent collection," Scarlett said. Her attention switched to Winnie. "Did you get the inventory list from Beatrix Morrow?"

"Sorry I forgot to mention it," Winnie answered. "It's in my office. Unfortunately, it's only a list of items. There are no notes about who owns them."

"It sounds as if we need to talk to Beatrix," Scarlett said. "And probably Sayed as well. I'm going to need proper paperwork for this collection. Devon must have had that."

"How did Devon handle paperwork on artifacts in the past?" Luke asked.

"I have no idea," Scarlett said. "These are the first new artifacts since I took the job. Winnie, were you ever involved with that?"

"It's outside my area, so I don't know how Devon handled paperwork," Winnie said. "But I'm certain that he would have never done anything shady."

"I agree," Luke said. "But it would help to check on past paperwork and know exactly what the past says about the present."

"I'll see what I can do," Scarlett said, desperately hoping that she wouldn't discover anything irregular.

Scarlett and Luke finished in the storage room, and Winnie returned to her office.

Scarlett felt a mix of relief and something like disappointment when Luke left with the scrap of linen in tow, her tests on it finished.

As she watched him leave, she had the thought that everything about the man was throwing her off-balance. She longed for the simplicity of facing a task she understood and losing herself in the process of work. Some of her tension eased when she got to the office and waded through files until late in the evening, taking only the briefest of breaks when Winnie popped in with a sandwich.

"Thank you," Scarlett said, accepting the snack. "I'm starving."

"I suspected you'd forgotten to eat," Winnie said. "And I wanted to let you know that the police didn't locate any paperwork on the artifacts in Devon's cabin on the ship."

"How did you find that out?" Scarlett asked. She unwrapped the sandwich and took a bite.

"Connections in the police department." Winnie gestured at the pad where Scarlett had been making notes. "Have you learned anything about past paperwork?"

"Yeah, Devon's record-keeping was flawless, and so was the previous curator's," Scarlett said. "Which makes the void for these artifacts even stranger."

"What will you do next?" Winnie asked.

"I'm not sure. Maybe something will come to me tonight."

"Well, don't stay too late," Winnie advised. "Exhaustion doesn't sharpen anyone's brain."

After Winnie left, Scarlett finished the sandwich and dug through more files, but nothing she read gave her any new insights. She drew a box on the pad where she'd been making notes and began listing people who could know more about the artifacts. She wrote in both Sayed and Beatrix. Then she added the museum in Cairo. They would know about the artifacts they had sent. After that, she noted a few connections of her own to help with tracking down the history of some of the most impressive pieces, if they didn't come from the Egyptian museum.

"I'll need to make some calls tomorrow," she said.

Her head pounded, and she suspected fatigue was playing a part in that. Scarlett needed to go home, spend time with Cleo, and get to bed. She switched off her computer and rose, reaching for her handbag.

The phone on her desk rang, and she picked up the receiver.

"Reed got what he deserved," a gruff male voice said.

"Who are you?" Scarlett asked, her hands trembling.

The man on the phone ignored the question, and his response made Scarlett's skin crawl. In a deep, husky whisper, he said, "He got what he deserved, and you will too."

10

The sun was setting by the time Scarlett shuffled to her front door, feeling oddly numb from exhaustion and the worry of a long day. With the museum closed, she should have arrived home early, but she'd gotten so caught up in the hunt for information on the artifacts she'd discovered in the crates that time had slipped away from her. She'd probably still be working if she could go any farther without help.

After fumbling with the key for longer than she cared to admit, Scarlett opened the door.

Cleo waited at the door and offered a chorus of complaints. The cat did not appreciate disruptions to her routine.

Scarlett scooped Cleo up for a hug, then buried her face in the cat's soft fur. "You needn't bother to scold me. I know the automatic feeder took care of you. It's not as if I was starving you."

Cleo stared at her.

Scarlett's stomach growled loudly, reminding her that the sandwich Winnie had brought her hours ago hadn't been large. "Fine. We'll share a snack, but don't expect this to become a regular thing. Neither of us wants to get into the habit of eating so late."

Though Scarlett doubted Cleo agreed with a prohibition on snacking at night, the cat snuggled closer.

Scarlett set Cleo down in the kitchen, washed her hands, and fixed a tuna sandwich. As she worked, she thought of the call she'd received and the police's response to it. "They figure all the publicity brings out the kooks. To be honest, I didn't find talk of kooks all that comforting."

Cleo meowed in what Scarlett chose to interpret as agreement.

Scarlett dropped a pinch of tuna into Cleo's food bowl, then leaned on the counter to eat the sandwich. She'd swallowed only a single bite when she heard a knock at the door.

She wasn't expecting anyone, and it was a little late even for Allie, her most regular drop-in caller. Still, if Allie was grieving Devon, she may have decided it was worth bending social norms.

Scarlett set her plate on the counter. With the burglary and the disturbing phone call weighing on her, she crept toward the door as if it might be a bomb.

She leaned toward the peephole at exactly the same moment Cleo swished by her leg and the person on the other side of the door knocked again. The combination made Scarlett flinch, which immediately made her feel ridiculous. "I've been all over the world," she whispered sternly to herself. "I am *not* afraid of my own front door."

As a result of her fierce resolve, Scarlett didn't check the peephole again. She simply threw open the door.

A man about her age leaped backward, obviously startled by the abruptness of the door opening. He was tall and slender with tight, dark curls and dark eyes. She'd never seen him before.

"If you're a reporter," she snapped, "I have nothing to say."

His expression turned faintly hostile. "I am not a reporter. I'm Peter Vore. I was Devon Reed's assistant."

"Oh," Scarlett said, immediately repentant for her hostile reception. "I'm sorry. You wouldn't believe the number of reporters who've been besieging the museum."

"I believe I can imagine it well enough," Peter said, his tone cool. "May I come in?"

She folded her arms over her chest, annoyed at his attitude. He was the one on her doorstep. "Isn't it a little late to be visiting someone you don't know?"

"I just arrived in Crescent Harbor, and I didn't want to wait until tomorrow," he replied. "Devon Reed was my employer, and he was also my good friend. I find it rather suspicious that he died in a town he has visited hundreds of times, and the only difference to this visit was you."

Scarlett narrowed her eyes. She could feel her temper rising with each word out of the man's mouth. Her dad had often advised her to learn to control the temper that had come with her red hair, and most of the time she managed it. This wasn't most of the time. "It is my understanding that Devon Reed was your *former* employer."

"I don't see what that has to do with anything," Peter said.

"And I don't see what my status at the museum has to do with Devon's death," she replied. "How did you even find out where I live?"

"I was Devon's assistant for many years," he answered. "Part of my job was tracking things down. I'd have been a sorry assistant if I couldn't locate one woman in a town as small as Crescent Harbor."

"Congratulations on your skills," Scarlett said. "You are welcome to come to the museum tomorrow when I am in my office. The museum will still be closed, but I'm sure you can get security to let you in. After all, that's probably one of your assistant skills." She began to swing the door closed.

Peter stuck his foot in the crack. "I demand to know what's going on here."

"Your role as former assistant to the late Devon Reed doesn't actually entitle you to any demands. I'll be happy to speak to you during museum hours." Scarlett gave his foot a sharp kick away from the door and found his groan gratifying. She closed the door with a satisfying thump.

"Don't think you've heard the last of me!" he shouted through the door.

With a sigh, Scarlett turned her back on the man, the door, and her long day. She wished she could be optimistic enough to think she'd heard the last of any of the unpleasant people she'd met lately.

She walked to the kitchen to finish her sandwich, only to find the siren call of tuna had proved too much for her usually well-behaved cat. The plate was little more than a ruin of bread scraps. The bite of sandwich Scarlett had gotten before answering the door was all she was getting.

After a surprisingly deep and dreamless sleep, Scarlett woke to sunlight streaming in through her windows, coloring her white bed linens almost golden.

She stretched, annoying Cleo who was sleeping on top of the comforter near Scarlett's knees, and surveyed her bright room. She loved the driftwood tables and the driftwood sculpture on the wall. It gave the room a summer vacation air that she enjoyed. When she'd made her design choices, she'd even thought of the museum job as a kind of holiday from the dirt and sweatiness of an archaeological dig.

Scarlett swung her legs off the bed and hopped up with a return of her usual energy. She refused to give in to anything pessimistic on such a beautiful Saturday morning. She'd go to the office and begin digging up answers. After all, it was what she was trained to do. She was an archaeologist, and it was time she acted like one.

She kept the positive determination through her shower, breakfast, and the drive to the museum. She was delighted to see the press had even thinned out a bit, though they were far from missing completely. As she strode through the museum, offering cheerful greetings to the security staff she passed, she settled on a game plan for the day. She would start by calling Hershel Smythe, the museum's previous curator.

Her work the previous night had proven that Hershel and Devon were both meticulous about paperwork on the items in the museum's collection. But searching through the files didn't reveal how the papers made the trip to the museum. Did they travel with shipments? Did Devon normally send them ahead? Or did he bring them himself? Any of the three options were possible, but only the previous curator could tell her for certain.

When Scarlett reached the second floor, she passed her own office door on a whim and headed for the special exhibit room. The night before, she'd instructed the workers to resume setting up the exhibit, and now she wondered if Luke would be there with Max.

The moment she opened the door, she heard voices inside. Max Northrup and Phillip Bentley stood just inside the exhibit.

"I'm so glad to see you," Max said to her. "I have some questions about the exhibit. Are there any changes in what you want?"

"Not at the moment," Scarlett said. "I'm hoping the police can find the mummy, but even if not, we have the coffin and more than enough artifacts for the exhibit." She scanned the area. "Is Luke helping?"

"Not today." Max clapped his companion on the shoulder. "Phillip decided to show up."

Phillip frowned at Max. "I wasn't feeling well," he told Scarlett.

"I'm sorry to hear that," Scarlett said, though the expression on Max's face suggested he doubted Phillip's explanation. Did Max think Phillip was merely playing hooky on the days he'd been absent?

Phillip was always so quiet that Scarlett didn't know much about him, but Max had worked with him. She made a mental note to ask Max some pointed questions later. If Phillip was prone to shirking, Scarlett wouldn't employ him for future exhibits.

"Are we good to continue?" she asked Max.

He smiled. "Good as gold."

"Excellent." Scarlett edged out the door and headed toward her office, then decided to check in with Winnie first. Winnie would be able to give her an update on anything she had heard from the police, and she'd almost certainly have contact information for Hershel Smythe. Surprisingly, Scarlett had not found his address or phone number the night before. She supposed Hershel had never felt the need to note his own contact information.

She descended the stairs, feeling foolish for not speaking with Winnie as soon as she'd arrived. Of course, Scarlett could call Winnie and ask her to stop by the office, but she decided the trot down the steps was rather invigorating.

When she entered the lobby, she glanced toward Burial Grounds and saw Allie sitting on a bench outside the coffee shop with Greta. Scarlett assumed Allie had come in to keep the security staff properly caffeinated, but she couldn't guess why Greta was present. With a lurch of concern, she worried that the staff might be thinking they were going to open already. How had she overlooked important details of her actual job? Scarlett suppressed a moan, then drew herself up and headed for the women.

Allie waved at Scarlett. "Need coffee?" she asked, jumping to her feet.

"Are mummies heartless?" Scarlett quipped, intending to keep it light. It wouldn't do staff morale any good if she got a reputation for being a stressed-out mess.

Allie blinked at her. "Huh?"

"Sorry," Scarlett said. "It's an old archaeologist joke. And yes, they are. I'd love coffee."

"Coming right up." Allie went inside the shop and bustled behind the counter.

Greta stood and walked over to Scarlett.

Bracing herself, Scarlett prepared to fess up for letting the docent think she needed to come to the museum today.

"How are you?" Greta asked with a gentle smile. "This must be a stressful time."

The question was so on the nose that it distracted Scarlett from the speech she was readying in her head. "I imagine it's less so for me than pretty much anyone else. I never had a chance to get terribly attached to Devon."

Greta's smile slipped away, and she took a sip of her coffee. "That's true, and I'm sorry for it. You would have enjoyed knowing him."

"I'm sure you're right," Scarlett said.

"Have you made any decisions about the museum?" Greta asked. "When it will open and whether you'll continue with the special exhibit?"

"The answer is yes to both," Scarlett said, feeling a prick of guilt for not communicating this to the staff before now. "We'll reopen on Monday. We have a school group coming, and I don't want them to miss out. And I've restarted work on the exhibit. I'm not completely sure what I'll do about the missing mummy, but I believe we'll have an exciting exhibit anyway. You don't think that's insensitive to Devon's death, do you?"

Greta shook her head. "Devon would have insisted on it. He would want people to see the incredible items he'd collected. He was always so proud of them."

Scarlett was touched anew at the woman's kindness. "I'm sorry that I haven't been more decisive about the opening. I assume you came in today because you thought we might be open. I shouldn't have left any confusion."

Greta patted her arm. "I'm not confused. Winnie called everyone. It's okay to let your staff carry some of the load, you know."

"You knew the museum was going to be closed?" Scarlett asked. Then a thought hit her. Greta assumed Scarlett needed her moral support.

"Of course," Greta replied. "I came in with Hal so I could take a peek at the terrific maze Max is building. Max asked Hal for his opinion on the faux rock finish, and I think the visitors will love it."

Scarlett nearly sagged with relief that Greta's presence had a logical explanation. "Max is doing an amazing job, and I know Luke helped with it too. I wish we could have the maze lead to the mummy as I'd intended, instead of taking visitors to an empty sarcophagus."

"It could lead to *a* mummy, even if it's not *the* mummy," Greta said with a twinkle in her eye. "I know Hal and Max learned a lot about making fake mummies while they were constructing tombs."

Scarlett considered the suggestion. It sounded a little theatrical for a museum, but it would most likely be effective. And anything that made visitors happy was a good thing. She could always include information about the real mummy. "I'll think about it. Thanks for the idea."

"Always glad to help," Greta said before taking another sip of her coffee.

"Have you seen Winnie this morning?" Scarlett asked. "I want to ask her for contact information for Hershel Smythe."

"You don't need Winnie for that," Greta said. "I can give it to you."

"That's great," Scarlett said. "Do you know Hershel well?"

"Hal and I used to socialize with him, but we haven't seen him in a while. I imagine he's embracing the quiet of retirement." Greta removed a notepad and a pen from the pocket of her jacket and jotted down the information. She tore out the page and handed it to Scarlett.

"Thank you." Scarlett folded the paper and slipped it into her pocket. She smiled. "You're a full-service docent."

Greta laughed. "We aim to please. Oh, and I did see Winnie earlier. She mentioned she needed to find you."

Scarlett groaned. Winnie had probably been waiting in her office when Scarlett had breezed right by the door. "As much as I enjoy a good comedy of errors, I should run upstairs and catch Winnie before she gives up and returns to the security office."

"Not without your coffee," Allie called as she exited the coffee shop with a cup. "If you're going to run around, you'll need the energy."

"Thanks." Scarlett accepted the cup and hurried to the stairs. As she walked across the open space, she felt as if she'd forgotten something. It was something to do with Allie, but she couldn't remember. She decided it would come to her later.

She picked up her pace to shake off that nagging sense of a memory tugging at the back of her mind. *At least I'm getting my exercise in.* She pulled her phone from her pocket and called Winnie to see if she was in Scarlett's office or her own.

The call went straight to voice mail.

"That's weird," Scarlett muttered.

She trotted to her office and noticed the door stood slightly ajar. She shoved it the rest of the way open, hoping to surprise whoever was inside. She did.

Phillip Bentley spun around and gaped at her.

Scarlett barely registered him because her attention was immediately drawn to the floor at Phillip's feet.

The floor where Winnie lay in a crumpled heap.

11

"This is not how it looks," Phillip insisted as he jumped away from Winnie's unmoving body on the floor.

Scarlett ignored him and rushed to Winnie's side, dropping to her knees beside the prone woman. She pressed her fingers to Winnie's throat, and a wash of relief swept through her when she felt a steady pulse. Scarlett heard Phillip leave the office, but she paid him no attention.

Scarlett located an oozing wound on Winnie's head. Since Winnie's pupils were equal and she was breathing fine, Scarlett felt safe to rock back on her heels, pull out her phone, and call for an ambulance.

After Scarlett disconnected the call, she noticed that Winnie was beginning to stir. "Take it easy," Scarlett cautioned. "You've had a nasty knock on the head."

Winnie groaned and struggled to sit up.

Scarlett gently held her down. "No, stay still until medical help gets here. A crack on the head hard enough to knock you out is no small thing."

"Did you catch the guy?" Winnie asked.

Scarlett was relieved to hear Winnie's voice sounded clear. "You saw a guy?"

Winnie started to shake her head, then moaned as she apparently realized what a bad idea that was. She raised a slightly shaky hand, but she didn't actually touch the wound. "I came up here to speak to you. I saw movement, but that's all. Then someone hit me with something."

"Could it have been Phillip Bentley?" Scarlett asked.

Winnie closed her eyes. "It could have been anyone. I didn't get a good glimpse of the person." She opened her eyes. "Why do you think it might be Phillip Bentley?"

"He was in here when I arrived," Scarlett said. "Standing over you."

Winnie closed her eyes again. "I hope you're going to fire him."

"Not until I'm sure he hit you," Scarlett said. "It's possible he only found you." Though if that were the case, why would he leave?

"I should tell my people to search for him," Winnie said.

Scarlett shook her head. "You should stay still."

Scarlett was grateful that the ambulance crew and the police arrived before Winnie's arguments managed to wear her down. As much as Scarlett was glad that Winnie was regaining a little strength and could think and speak clearly, she knew better than to let her head of security get up before she was examined. A concussion would be bad, but Scarlett knew there were worse possibilities.

As Scarlett expected, the ambulance crew said Winnie needed to go to the hospital. And equally as expected, Winnie protested.

"Stop that," Scarlett ordered. "I need my head of security in top shape, so go along to the hospital or you're fired."

"Bully," Winnie accused, but she didn't resist anymore.

That worried Scarlett. Winnie must have been hurting if she gave in so easily.

"Miss McCormick." The police officer had waited patiently while Scarlett's sole attention had been on Winnie, but now he held a notepad and a pen. "Are you ready to tell me what happened?"

Scarlett sighed. She wished she could go straight to the hospital where she could focus on fretting over Winnie's condition, but she knew she needed to tell the police what she saw.

She turned to the police officer. She recognized the short, stocky man immediately as the one who'd directed her at the huge cargo ship.

It took another moment for her to come up with his name. "We meet again, Officer Young."

He brightened a bit, evidently pleased that she'd remembered. "I get around. Tell me about how Miss Varma received her injury. I'll be questioning her at the hospital, but it won't be until the doctor has seen her."

"She told me she didn't see anyone, only a flash of motion before someone hit her," Scarlett said. "I did see someone, but I don't know if it's the person who attacked her."

"Who was it?" Young asked, scribbling in his notepad. "And when?"

Scarlett explained that she'd gone to her office because she'd been told Winnie was searching for her. "I walked in on Phillip Bentley standing over her. I didn't notice anything in his hands, so if he hit her, he must have gotten rid of the weapon."

"Did he speak to you?" the officer asked.

"Only to say that it wasn't what it looked like," Scarlett answered. "He left as soon as I knelt down to examine Winnie."

Young jotted down more notes. "What's your relationship to Phillip Bentley?"

"Employer," she said. "I hired him to work on the special exhibit room. He's a handyman."

"We'll track him down and ask what he knows," the officer assured her.

"You might want to chat with Max Northrup as well," Scarlett said. "He's been working closely with Phillip. I have contact information for both of them. If you can wait a second, I'll find it."

"That would be helpful," Young said. "While you're hunting for the information, can you make sure nothing is missing from your office? Miss Varma might have been attacked because she surprised a thief."

Scarlett couldn't believe she hadn't considered that possibility. Her concern for Winnie must have distracted her from the obvious. She went through her desk and nearby bookcases. She didn't see anything missing and said as much before she switched on her computer and collected the contact information for Max and Phillip. "Max is probably going to be in the special exhibit room, if you want to talk to him right away."

"But you're convinced nothing is stolen," Officer Young pressed.

"As sure as I can be without a thorough check," she said.

"Call us if you find something when you do that." He smiled widely for the first time. "Now, since you suggested it, I'm going to go speak with Max Northrup. I like the idea of a sneak peek of the special exhibit."

"There's nothing much in place yet," Scarlett warned him.

"That's okay. I have a good imagination." Young flipped his notebook closed. "I'll keep you in the loop, and you do the same."

After the officer left, Scarlett studied her office once more, but she couldn't imagine what someone would want to steal. She had a few small pieces she'd collected on her travels, but most of those were in her home. The home that had been broken into. Could the two incidents be related? If so, what could someone possibly be searching for?

With the police gone, Scarlett resisted the urge to call the hospital since there hadn't been enough time for Winnie to be examined, especially if tests were involved. She spent some time searching for background on the artifacts she'd logged, but she had difficulty concentrating.

Finally, Scarlett gave in to her impatience and phoned the hospital. Though she didn't exactly get a thorough update, she learned that Winnie would probably be staying overnight. It was also strongly suggested that the injured woman needed rest, not visitors.

After the call, Scarlett felt even more restless, so she decided to drive over to Hershel Smythe's house and ask the former curator about the previous procedures for artifact delivery.

The address wasn't far from the museum, which made sense. The man probably preferred a short commute to work. The white stucco house was small, but it had a stunning view of the Pacific Ocean. Scarlett could hear the waves crashing in the distance as she got out of her car.

The door opened before she had a chance to ring the bell. The sight of the elderly man was a shock. Though Scarlett had never met him, no one had mentioned Hershel was ill, and the man before her definitely was. His skin was a sickly sallow color, and his clothing fit loosely, as if bought for a stouter man.

"I saw you pull in," Hershel explained. He took a step away from the door. "Please come in, Miss McCormick."

She blinked at him. "You know who I am?"

"I saw your photo before Devon hired you, and your hair is rather distinctive," he said. "Plus, I have an excellent memory for faces. Please come in. I cannot stand for long periods of time these days."

Scarlett followed him inside. The house had plenty of windows, but dark curtains kept the light low.

"Forgive the shadows," Hershel said, almost as if he could read her mind. "Bright light tends to give me headaches."

She followed him into a cozy and scrupulously clean sitting room.

He waved at a love seat. "Can I get you something? I don't drink coffee, but I could make you a cup of tea."

"I'm fine," Scarlett said as she perched on the edge of the love seat's cushion. "I wanted to speak with you about the museum's inventory acquisition procedures."

Hershel sank into a nearby recliner. "Of course. And let me apologize for not coming to the museum to meet you when you started the job.

I did help Devon choose you as the new curator. I was impressed by the work you did in New York."

"Thank you. That's kind of you." She studied the man's lined face. "Greta speaks warmly of you, by the way. In fact, all the staff does."

His eyes lit up. "I don't know what I would have done without Greta and Hal. They are amazing docents and truly fine people."

"I completely agree," Scarlett said.

"I received a mailer about your upcoming special exhibit," Hershel remarked. "You'll have to ask Devon to come see me when he gets to town. I miss our spirited conversations about antiquities."

She winced. "You must not follow the news."

He chuckled. "No, I'm afraid I find it all terribly disheartening. When you get to be my age, the way history repeats itself begins to feel more dispiriting than academic."

"I imagine so." Scarlett reached out and rested a hand on top of his gnarled fingers. "I'm sorry to tell you this, but Devon has died."

"Oh no." The elderly man's eyes filled with tears, and he seemed to grow even paler.

"Is there anyone I can call to be here with you?" she asked. "Family perhaps?"

Hershel waved away her concern. "I'm fine. It's a shock, but I suppose I should be getting used to loss. I lost my daughter years ago and my wife well before that. But I am not alone. I have a grandson, and he will be by later. He drops in most days."

"That's good," Scarlett said, though she wished the grandson would arrive right away.

"Please don't worry," he said. "Let's speak of other things. You had questions about procedures?"

"Yes, specifically paperwork," she replied. "When Devon acquired new items for the museum, did they ever arrive without paperwork?

Was he in the habit of bringing the paperwork with him?"

"There were manifests," the retired curator said. "Devon usually sent papers ahead, so I already knew the history of each piece long before they arrived." He frowned. "Why do you ask? Is there a problem?"

"Yes, or at least an irregularity," Scarlett said. "I've received a shipment from Egypt that arrived with no papers at all. And with Devon's death, I'm at a loss to track some of the items."

"That's strange," Hershel said. "Shipping art and artifacts from Egypt is a paperwork-heavy procedure. The papers must have existed at some point, and these days, there should be copies."

She managed a smile, hoping to calm the man's distress on her behalf. "I'm sure you're right, and I shouldn't overstay my welcome and wear you out."

"Alas, I do wear out easily, even though I have enjoyed the visit of the new curator tremendously." He sighed. "I wish you didn't have such tragic news. Was Devon's death some sort of accident? As far as I knew, his health was excellent."

"I'm afraid the police suspect someone killed him," Scarlett said. "Can you think of any enemies Mr. Reed may have had?"

Hershel shook his head, making his sparse fluff of hair bounce. "None that I can think of. Devon was a kind man and a good friend, but he was also intensely private. If he were having trouble, I'm not sure he would have confided in me."

She changed the subject and chatted for a few moments about things she admired about the museum, hoping to pull the elderly man's thoughts in a more pleasant direction. To her relief, his extreme pallor lessened. She thanked him for his time and left.

When Scarlett stepped outside, she was nearly dazzled by the bright sunlight after the shadowy dimness in the house. She blinked and waited for her vision to adjust before heading for the car, frustrated that the visit hadn't clarified anything. Why was the paperwork missing for the exhibits? Why were people connected to the museum being targeted?

And where could she go for answers?

12

When Scarlett got home from Hershel's house, she tried to sit on the sectional for the usual session of Cleo petting, but she was too fidgety to settle.

Cleo apparently noticed her restlessness. She hopped down from the sofa and glared at Scarlett before stalking away.

"Sorry about that," she called after the annoyed cat.

Scarlett stood and started pacing. She ended up in the kitchen, leaning over the counter and doodling on a notepad. The past few days made no sense, but Scarlett knew it had to be because something was missing. She flipped over the scribbled-on sheet of paper and began sketching a timeline. She focused on the last four days, but she soon realized the weirdness had begun much earlier so the timeline should too.

It was plain that someone had a problem with Scarlett's hiring, but who? Obviously, it had to be someone associated with the museum. She didn't believe it was Hershel. From her conversation with the retired curator, it sounded as if choosing Scarlett had been a joint decision. She also suspected illness may have played a part in the suddenness of Hershel's retirement.

Maybe whoever was upset about her hiring didn't know that Hershel was ill. Or maybe it was someone who thought a different person should have been hired. She contemplated the people she'd met, people she now considered friends.

Scarlett quickly rejected Allie as a suspect. She was Scarlett's best friend in Crescent Harbor. In fact, if Allie wasn't dealing with her own pain over Devon's death, she'd probably be at Scarlett's house right now, helping her solve this mystery.

She also couldn't think of any reason Winnie would be upset that Scarlett had been hired. Winnie hadn't been quite as friendly as Allie, but she wasn't hostile either. Plus, there was no way Winnie could have taken the curator job. She wasn't qualified.

Then Scarlett had a sudden, upsetting thought. There was only one person at the museum who could have handled the job of curator: Greta. It would have been a challenge for the woman, but she was a historian and a former college professor, so she would have handled all the paperwork perfectly well.

Scarlett tried to picture Greta plotting the deliveries of wilting flowers and threatening notes, but her imagination simply wouldn't stretch that far. Greta was kind and friendly, but she was also a direct person. If she had a problem with Scarlett, she would have simply said so.

What if it was someone taking up what he considered Greta's offense? Maybe Hal believed his wife wanted the job or should have had it. Now that Scarlett thought about it, wilting flowers and menacing notes were theatrical acts. Hal had been solicitous and warm, but he was also a professional actor. How hard would it have been to put on a caring face when he actually wished Scarlett ill?

With a groan, Scarlett pushed the notepad aside. Her theory sort of fit, but it didn't feel right. Even if Hal had hopes of Greta getting the job, Scarlett couldn't imagine either of the cheerful docents killing someone and stuffing him into a mummy case. Of course, that assumed Devon's death and the flowers were related. If they were, what if they had nothing to do with Scarlett's job? She assumed they did because the florist card called her a usurper, but what if it meant something else?

Still, if the whole thing was related to the mummy exhibit somehow, did the timeline fit? She knew a collection as large as the one for the exhibit didn't come together quickly. Devon had been working on the project before he ever mentioned it to her, maybe even before he hired her.

"Devon didn't tell me about it until my second week on the job," she said aloud.

This time Cleo responded to her voice and padded over to peer up at her.

"He didn't sound worried during that call," Scarlett continued. "He was excited."

Cleo meowed in response.

Scarlett pretended that Cleo was challenging her premise. "He must have had some of the artifacts by then," she explained to the cat. "And I talked to him directly only once more. He didn't sound worried then either." Did he? Would she have even noticed? She'd mostly focused on what she needed to do.

"No offense, sweet girl," she told the cat, "but I need to talk to a human. I also need to find out if Winnie is okay." She grabbed her car keys and headed for the door, eliciting a response from Cleo that sounded like complaints, but Scarlett only patted the cat and left.

Once in the car, she realized she should have called first, so before she even buckled in, she rang Winnie's phone.

Her head of security answered immediately. "What's going on?"

"Oh, it's good to hear your voice," Scarlett said. "Are you okay? Are you at the hospital?"

"Yes and no," Winnie said. "I decided not to stay. The doctors weren't thrilled, but I'm fine. I have a headache, but it isn't too bad. I should be at work on Monday."

"Please don't worry about that," Scarlett said. "Can I bring dinner around? I could get tacos from Rosita's, if you're up for it." She hoped Winnie was, because Scarlett had realized she was hungry and Rosita's Mexican Restaurant was one of her favorites.

"That would be great," Winnie said. "I was trying to think what I should make for supper, and cooking sounded exhausting."

Already feeling more optimistic now that she had something to do, Scarlett fastened her seat belt and started the car. She spotted Cleo staring at her from the window and silently promised the cat she'd bring her a fish taco.

After picking up the order, Scarlett drove to Winnie's apartment building. It was sandwiched between a glassblower's studio and the Greek to Me Playhouse. When Scarlett searched for a parking spot, she located one near the playhouse. It was going to be a bit of a hike to Winnie's place, but Scarlett didn't mind. It would help her work off some of her restless energy. As she grabbed the takeout bag, it stirred up even more of the delicious aromas from the food. Scarlett's stomach growled in anticipation.

Scarlett pressed her hand against her stomach. "Hush now. You'll have to be patient."

After she swung open the car door and climbed out, she regarded the playhouse. The theater kept popping into her museum experiences lately. As she'd noted earlier, Hal was an actor and a director there. Her handyman for the new exhibit had brought techniques he'd gained from making sets for a play. And Greta had even suggested fabricating a mummy for the new exhibit, using more theater techniques.

"Coincidence?" Scarlett whispered. She couldn't say, but the thought of adding one more element to this situation depressed her. She turned her back on the playhouse and walked to Winnie's apartment.

When Winnie answered the door, Scarlett immediately saw that her friend was pale and the headache pain showed in her eyes. Clearly, it wasn't as mild as Winnie had claimed.

Winnie waved her in and took an exaggerated sniff. "The tacos smell fantastic. You're a lifesaver."

"And you should be sitting down," Scarlett chided gently.

"My head does ache a little," Winnie admitted as she led Scarlett to a tall table and stools.

As Scarlett set out the tacos, chips, guacamole, and drinks, she admired the industrial vibe of the loft apartment and Winnie's decorating. Like Winnie herself, the overall impression was no-nonsense simplicity with a dash of unexpected elegance.

When the food was spread out, Scarlett was startled by a fluttering sound and jumped as a bird flew past her head to land on one of the stools. "Oh, you have a parrot."

"Yes, and he loves a grand entrance." Winnie rubbed the parrot under his beak, and the bird shut his eyes and leaned into it. "This is Mac."

"Does he always fly free?" Scarlett asked.

"When I'm home," Winnie said. She raised an eyebrow at the bird. "But he knows better than to be scaring guests."

If Mac understood the reproof, he showed no sign. He was too busy staring at the food.

"Yes, I'll give you a bit of tortilla," Winnie told the parrot. "But you have to be good."

When Scarlett and Winnie settled at the table, with Mac watching from his perch on the stool, they ate while chatting about inconsequential things. Scarlett was relieved to see some of Winnie's paleness subside as they worked their way through the delicious meal.

Since Winnie appeared recovered enough for more pointed conversation, Scarlett said, "Before I came here, I went to see Hershel Smythe."

Winnie's face lit up. "How is he? I always felt as if Hershel couldn't be unpleasant if he tried."

"He was gracious and kind, but he was also visibly ill," Scarlett said. "He didn't mention what was bothering him, and I didn't feel it was my place to ask."

"Oh, that's awful," Winnie said. "I didn't realize he wasn't well. Though he had been losing weight in the last month or so before he retired. I remember joking with him about slimming down for an active retirement." She sighed. "Now I feel terrible that I haven't been by to see him. I'll go tomorrow after church."

"Maybe you could focus on your own recovery and stay home at least for a day or two," Scarlett suggested. "I think both Hershel and the church will be fine while you take it easy."

"I do still have a headache," Winnie said. "I want to know who knocked me out, so I can return the favor."

"Are you sure you didn't see anyone?" Scarlett asked.

Winnie started to shake her head, then winced. "No, I thought your office was empty. The person must have been hiding behind the door, and I missed him." She huffed in frustration. "I'm not usually so inattentive."

"You had no reason to consider my office potentially dangerous," Scarlett said. She hated to see Winnie upset, especially since her friend should be resting and recovering, not blaming herself. Scarlett decided to try a distraction. "So, what brought you to my office in the first place?"

"I came to tell you what I learned about Sayed Kamal. I spoke with someone on the phone who worked with him in Cairo."

Scarlett straightened. "That's excellent."

"He described Sayed to me," Winnie continued. "I'm certain the man we've been dealing with is indeed Sayed Kamal. The physical description matched, and the man I spoke with said that Sayed is considered a bit of a loose cannon because he's grown increasingly militant about what he perceives as British and American looting of Egyptian antiquities."

"That does sound like the man we've met," Scarlett agreed.

"Apparently, Sayed's employers have considered moving him to a different position because of this specific problem," Winnie said. "He would be transferred to a role with the museum that didn't interact with collectors of antiquities since he's been growing less and less diplomatic with each assignment."

Scarlett pondered the information. Perhaps if the higher-ups had acted on that, it would have stopped the events leading to Devon's death. Then she pushed the idea aside. It was conjecture at this point. No matter how much Sayed hated antiquities collectors, there was no reason to think he'd killed one. She said as much to Winnie.

"You may be right," Winnie said. "The man I spoke with said that a meeting about the subject of moving Sayed to a different department is what kept him in Cairo and made him miss traveling with the mummy on the cargo ship. That's why Sayed had to fly instead."

"That's one question answered," Scarlett said. "It also possibly explains Sayed's ongoing bad mood. If his feelings about antiquities fuel a personal crusade, he probably wouldn't appreciate being transferred to a position that doesn't deal with them."

"True," Winnie said. "According to my source, right after the meeting, Sayed was extremely angry. In fact, my source said he appeared *murderous*."

An icy chill ran up Scarlett's spine as she wondered if that description was entirely too accurate.

13

On Sunday morning, Scarlett stood next to a polished oak pew in Grace Church. She held an open hymnal, but she wasn't singing. Instead, she let the beautiful voices of the other congregants wash over her and soothe the stress of the last few days.

Though many people sang the traditional hymn, it was easy to pick out the booming voice of Chief Rodriguez rolling toward Scarlett from the choir. Scarlett admired the way he threw himself into each song. He obviously loved to sing, and that joy rang out in each note.

Scarlett's own surety did not meet the chief's, but she finally joined in the singing and gave as much of herself to the hymn as she could. She hoped the words of faith would help push away all the questions and worries that kept crowding into her mind. She admired people who could be totally in the moment, but she couldn't claim to be one of them.

After the singing ended and Scarlett sat down on the pew, she scanned the congregation. As she did every week, she searched the pews for familiar faces. Each Sunday she recognized a few more people. She constantly met people at the museum and in the community. Of course, she couldn't put a name to every face, but now she could identify a few of the police officers she'd met recently. This habit was her way of gauging how much Crescent Harbor was becoming home. One day when most of the faces around her were familiar, she imagined she would finally feel settled.

The gentle voice of the pastor pulled her attention to the pulpit.

Pastor Russ Coleman warmly greeted the congregation. As Scarlett had admired the abandon with which Chief Rodriguez sang, she also admired the pastor's unshakable calm and unwavering kindness. Because of the example he set, Scarlett doubted anyone left Grace Church feeling unwelcome. She fondly remembered her own first visit. Pastor Coleman had made a point to introduce himself to her, asking surprisingly astute questions about archaeology, and his wife, Martha, had treated Scarlett as if she were an old friend.

Scarlett settled a bit deeper into the pew with a soundless sigh. This was exactly where she needed to be after her stressful week. The pastor's teaching on wisdom and peace spoke directly to her, touching on her own need for balance.

When the service ended and Scarlett stepped out of the church and into the bright sunlight, she was so relaxed that she didn't even jump when Allie stepped up to her side and linked an arm through hers.

"Sorry I didn't sit with you," Allie said. "I was running late, so I took a seat at the back. How are you doing?"

Scarlett was touched by the question, especially since it was Allie who'd suffered a loss. "I'm fine, but I'm worried about Winnie. I saw her yesterday evening for dinner, and I'm afraid that I may have worn her out."

"I called her this morning," Allie said as she dropped Scarlett's arm. "She's feeling much better, but she was going to take your advice and stay home today. She plans to be at work tomorrow."

Scarlett blinked. "I told her that she shouldn't feel as if she has to do that."

"Are you kidding?" Allie asked. "You couldn't keep Winnie away. She's extremely dedicated, not like me. If someone clunked me on the head, I'd use it as an excuse to kick back and surf for a week."

"Because getting knocked into the ocean over and over is so restful," Scarlett said with a chuckle.

Allie grinned. "It is if you're me. I did make Winnie promise to goof off and relax all day today. No work, no stress. She said the most strenuous thing on her agenda was petting Mac."

"Sounds good." Scarlett suddenly had a thought and realized what she had forgotten at the museum. *Peter Vore.* Feeling guilty for not mentioning it before now, she tried for a casual tone. "By the way, were you aware that Peter Vore is in town?"

"Peter?" Allie echoed, sounding shocked. "Are you sure? I can't imagine why he hasn't called me."

"He showed up at my house Friday night," Scarlett said. "He was extremely upset about Devon's death."

"Friday night?" Allie folded her arms over her chest. "And you didn't tell me yesterday?"

Scarlett cringed. "I honestly forgot. I'm sorry. A lot has been coming at me."

"I can understand that," Allie said, relaxing her posture. "It's okay. But I want to know why Peter didn't contact me. That's not like him."

Scarlett didn't comment because she didn't know Peter. On first impression, she hadn't found the man appealing at all. "If he gets in touch with you, be careful. I realize he must be upset, but he came across as rather aggressive."

Allie took a step back and studied Scarlett's face. "You actually mean that. Honestly, Peter wouldn't hurt me. He wouldn't hurt anyone. We've known each other for years."

Scarlett didn't want to argue, especially since she doubted she could make Allie take care. She wished her friend a good Sunday surf, which netted her another sunny smile. Then Scarlett headed for the parking lot, a little sad that much of her peaceful calm had slid into worry.

When she approached her Prius, she heard her name and spun around to see Luke waving at her.

He trotted toward her, weaving skillfully through the cars in the lot. When he reached her, he said, "I heard about Winnie. How is she doing?"

"I saw her yesterday after she came home from the hospital," Scarlett answered. "Allie talked to her today. She's home resting, and she insists that she'll be at work tomorrow."

"Winnie has always been determined," Luke said. "I'm glad she has both of you to keep her from overdoing it."

"Have you heard any other news?" she asked.

"I talked to the police yesterday afternoon," he answered. "I learned they tracked down the florist, but I couldn't find out the name of the sender. Apparently, the person prepaid in cash for weekly deliveries starting at the time you were hired."

"For how long?" Scarlett asked, wondering how many more she'd have to face.

"A couple of months," Luke said. "But the police put a stop to the deliveries."

"Did they discover why the flowers wilt as soon as I get them?"

"No, though I'm not sure they took the whole thing as seriously as I do, especially with a murder on their hands," he said. "I went to the florist right after I talked to the police and caught them before they closed. I was told the same thing as the police, but I suspect the florist knows more than she's saying. She struck me as off somehow."

"Could she simply have been freaked out by an FBI visit?"

Luke's expression lightened. "It's possible. Not everyone finds us easy to talk to."

"I can't imagine," she said with a grin.

"At any rate, I rescinded the police order to stop the deliveries," he said. "When the next one comes, I want to be there so we can test the flowers before they're put in water. Maybe they're coated with something that washes off."

Scarlett hated the thought of another delivery, but she agreed.

"I have one more request," Luke said. "Can I check out your kitchen and the backyard where the intruder entered and exited?"

She didn't answer immediately. She had been looking forward to a Sunday of cat snuggling and maybe a phone call with her mom. Something normal and free of stress.

Luke apparently noticed her hesitation, because he gave her what Scarlett was beginning to think of as his patented engaging smile and said, "I'll bring lunch."

She rolled her eyes to let him know the rather obvious attempt to charm her didn't work, though she did enjoy the smile. "Sure, since you're obviously not going to give up. But I must remind you that I have a cat. If you're allergic, you'll sneeze and itch. And I won't apologize for it."

"It's all right," he said. "I'm not allergic. I'll admit I'm more of a dog guy, but I don't have a problem with cats."

They arranged to meet at Scarlett's house, and she rattled off her address. He said he'd pick up the food on the way.

Scarlett was glad to hear it, but she made a mental promise to eat salad for a couple of days after two indulgences in a row. She was also glad of the chance to get home ahead of Luke's arrival. It would give her a few minutes to make sure there was nothing she'd be embarrassed for him to see, like one of the romantic mysteries she'd recently started reading and found she enjoyed.

Later when Luke rapped on the door, Scarlett scanned the front rooms. They were acceptably neat, so she scooped up Cleo, headed for the door, and opened it.

Luke laughed. "You wanted to prove you have a cat?"

"No, I wanted to be sure Cleo didn't dash out the open door," she replied. "We're still new enough here that the lure of an open door is a lot for a cat to resist."

"The lure of the unknown is a lot for me to resist, so I can relate." He held up two bags, both printed with a scruffy dog in a sea captain's hat, the logo of The Salty Dog. "I hope you don't mind fish and chips."

"I love them," Scarlett said, moving out of the way to let him in. "I've been trying to figure out the best place to get them in Crescent Harbor."

"The Salty Dog." Luke carried the bags to the kitchen counter. "No one else even comes close. The secret is in the batter."

"What is it?" she asked.

He grinned at her. "Now if everyone knew, it wouldn't be a secret, would it?"

She had almost expected Luke to leap into FBI mode and begin snooping around, but he chatted about good fish and chips while unloading the bags. He acted completely at ease and at home. Scarlett began collecting plates, forks, and napkins.

Luke gaped at her in mock horror. "Plates? Forks? My dear lady, fish and chips are best eaten with your hands straight from the takeout package."

She put the plates and forks down on the counter. "Well, I wouldn't want to violate local custom. Are napkins all right?"

"Of course," he replied. "There are some in the bag. I'm thorough."

"We should eat at the table in the dining room," Scarlett said. "You can see the rear door from there. Maybe you'll find a clue while you eat."

"I might," Luke said seriously. "I'm an extremely good FBI agent."

"And modest to a fault," she teased.

He grinned. "That too."

When they settled at the table with the food, Cleo watched them closely from beside the double French doors that led out to the patio.

The cat's attention was so focused that Scarlett suspected Cleo hoped some of the fish would leap her way. "You had fish yesterday," she told the cat.

Luke glanced up from dipping a hunk of cod in cocktail sauce. "You talk to your cat often?"

She raised her chin. "Yes, I do."

"I read somewhere that talking to pets is good for your blood pressure," he said. "It makes me sorry I don't have a dog, but I'm out of town so much with work that I couldn't do that. It would be cruel to the dog."

"I thought about that for a long time before I got Cleo," Scarlett said. "Since I do travel sometimes for work. When I worked for a museum in New York, my folks took Cleo whenever I had to travel." She shook her head. "And that cat always came home a little plumper. Mom can be a pushover."

"My folks live in San Diego," Luke said. "They'd be happy to watch a dog, but sometimes I get no advance warning before leaving town on a case. I suspect it would strain even my angelic mother if I dropped a dog off in the middle of the night."

"So, are you from San Diego?" she asked casually as she picked up a fry and dipped it in ketchup.

"Born and raised," he replied. "I got my master's in criminal justice and criminology from San Diego State University. I trained in Quantico, Virginia, after I joined the FBI, so I've spent some time on the East Coast too. What about you?"

"I was born and raised in Ithaca, New York," Scarlett said. "I received my master's in archaeology from Cornell." She chuckled. "We were a whole country apart."

"And yet, here we are." Luke grinned at her.

Scarlett wasn't quite sure how to respond. Before she could come up with another conversational topic, she noticed that Cleo no longer sat near the door. Scarlett scanned the room for the cat, suddenly picturing Cleo on the kitchen counter with her head in the delivery bag.

"Something wrong?" he asked.

"I was wondering where Cleo went." She stood to get a better view of the kitchen. "Cats can be like toddlers. When they're quiet, it sometimes means they're getting into mischief."

Cleo was in the kitchen, but she wasn't on the counter. Instead, Scarlett saw the cat batting something around on the floor. "Excuse me a second." She walked around the table and headed into the kitchen. As she got closer, she realized Cleo was chasing a wad of paper.

Scarlett felt a pang of embarrassment that the cat had found some trash in what she had thought was a neat house. She bent down and snatched up the paper.

"What's that?" Luke asked, following her.

She suppressed a groan. *So much for not letting him know I had trash on the floor.* "Nothing. Probably an old receipt or something I was using for a bookmark." As she spread out the crumpled paper, she drew in a sharp breath.

"What's wrong?" he asked.

Scarlett held up the paper to show him. It was covered with carefully copied hieroglyphics.

"My ancient Egyptian is a little rusty," Luke said. "Would you translate it for me?"

She pointed. "These are the 'usurper' hieroglyphics from the florist notes, but there's more here this time. I think this may be the link between the delivery flowers and Devon's murder."

"Do you want to share what else it says?" he asked.

Scarlett swallowed hard. "'Death to the usurper.'"

14

Scarlett shook her head, rejecting everything about the note she'd found. "So the break-in was merely to leave me another note? The wilting flowers sent to my office weren't enough? This person had to invade my home?" She recognized that her voice had grown a little strident, so she stopped talking.

Luke didn't comment as he slid the note into an evidence bag.

"Did you honestly carry an evidence bag to church?" she asked.

"I take at least one evidence bag pretty much everywhere," he said. "I've had to create makeshift evidence protection a few too many times when unexpected events pop up."

"You must live an interesting life."

Luke grinned. "It was *your* note."

Scarlett moaned. "You're right. When did my life take this weird turn?"

He left that question unanswered. "It's true that the intruder you saw probably dropped this note when you and Cleo appeared, but let's try not to make too many assumptions. If you don't mind, I want to search the house for signs of a second break-in. The note could have been left this morning when you were at church or anytime you were at work."

She wrapped her arms around herself. "That doesn't make me feel any better."

"It wasn't meant to," Luke admitted. "Can I snoop around?"

"Go ahead." Scarlett scooped up Cleo and followed him around the house as he examined the window and door locks, then prowled around the yard.

Finally, Luke seemed satisfied and announced that he'd discovered no sign of tampering with any of the locks. "I assume you've taken care to lock up since the intruder," he said as they went back inside.

"I have." She didn't mention that sometimes she checked her locks multiple times now.

"I think it's safe to say the note arrived with the previous intrusion," he concluded. "It's probable the intruder meant for it to be discovered much sooner."

"Cleo may have been hiding it," Scarlett suggested, giving Cleo a small hug to show she wasn't harboring hard feelings. "She collects bits of paper. I can't leave myself notes because they disappear into Cleo's stash, which I haven't been able to locate."

"You have an interesting roommate," Luke said. "But you might need something more than an attack cat and note thief. You should consider some alarms and maybe a few cameras."

Scarlett stiffened so much that Cleo squirmed in protest, so she set the cat down on the sectional in the living room. "I appreciate the advice, but I refuse to treat my home like a bunker. I have good locks, and I use them."

Luke's mouth tightened, but he didn't argue with her. "Do you know why someone might want to leave you messages like this?"

She waved a hand toward the kitchen where they'd found the note. "I think someone must be upset with me for taking Hershel's job. I suppose the person may even have blamed Devon because he hired me."

"Upset enough to kill Devon?" he asked skeptically.

His tone reflected her own doubts. Scarlett acknowledged that it seemed like a poor motive. "Would that be the oddest motive for murder you've ever heard?"

Luke winced. "No, but I'm not inclined to assume it's that simple. I like Hershel, and I know Devon was extremely fond of him. It's hard to believe he could have pushed Hershel out of a job."

"I met Hershel, and he's a nice man," she responded. "Plus, I don't think he's in any condition to make trouble for me. He isn't well."

"I'm sorry to hear that," he said. "Still, it's all the more reason to doubt he has anything to do with this."

"What if he's so nice someone thinks they're saving him? Maybe he had a weird secret admirer among the museum patrons. Someone smitten with him." Scarlett actually had trouble picturing anyone having a huge crush on the sickly man she'd met, but it was clear the decline in his health was recent. And she could easily imagine Hershel's courtly manners charming one of their patrons.

Luke raised his eyebrows. "I didn't know you had such romantic notions."

"I'm just trying to consider all the possibilities," she said. "Maybe it has nothing to do with Hershel or the job. Perhaps it's been about Devon all along, and the dying flowers were some kind of threat."

"What do you mean?"

"Dr. Sayed Kamal thinks Americans basically steal Egyptian antiquities," Scarlett explained. "In fact, he's apparently rabid about the idea. He might see the wealthy Americans, and Devon in particular, as trying to usurp Egyptian ownership of their own history. Maybe his anger over that blended with his anger over being pushed to a new assignment, and it set him off."

"That doesn't sound completely crazy," Luke admitted.

She fought the urge to make a snarky remark about weak praise.

"You could be right, and the notes were more about Devon than you," he continued. "But they showed up in your office and your home. You need to be careful."

"I *am* careful, but don't try to distract me." Scarlett had no intention of letting Luke drag the conversation away from Sayed now that she felt as if she'd finally found a logical suspect. "As far as I've seen, Sayed is the only person with a real motive. He was hostile about Devon bringing those antiquities to the States for display."

"I'm not shooting down the idea," Luke assured her. "I want to speak to the man. Unfortunately, the police say he's elusive. The hotel he gave as the place he was staying proved to be a lie, and it was a lie they didn't catch until after they'd released him. Now they don't know where he is."

"He does tend to appear and disappear," she said.

He was quiet, clearly deep in thought.

Scarlett edged around him and headed for the kitchen to make a cup of coffee. She could use one.

Remaining in the living room area, Luke pulled out his phone and placed a call.

Scarlett was annoyed to realize she couldn't hear what he was saying.

When he joined her in the kitchen, she handed him a mug of coffee. "Would it be too nosy if I asked what the call was about?"

"Putting the power of the FBI in motion," Luke said. "I expect we'll know the location of Dr. Kamal Sayed by the time this mug is empty."

"That's optimistic," Scarlett said.

"I'm always an optimist." He regarded the kitchen. "You're very neat."

"I am an archaeologist," she said. "Organization is baked into us."

Luke changed the subject to New York City. He'd visited only a few times, but he had definite preferences in the restaurants. They debated who made the best pizza until his phone rang.

The call was quick. When he disconnected, he swallowed the last of his coffee and announced, "Sayed is at the Harbor View Inn, which is conveniently close to the museum. I'm going over to chat with him. Do you want to come?"

Scarlett gaped at him. "You're taking an archaeologist along on your interview with a suspect?"

"You're an expert in the same field as the suspect," Luke reminded her. "Think of yourself as a consultant. Also, this chat is unofficial, but that's going to change if I don't like what he has to say."

"Then I'm in."

"Great. We'll take my car."

Scarlett felt a flash of the stubbornness she could sometimes be prey to since she didn't appreciate people making assumptions without asking, but it made sense. *I should get used to being a passenger. I've had to do it a lot lately.*

She locked up carefully before heading to Luke's black Volvo. To her surprise, when he opened the passenger door for her, the interior was black as well. "You must enjoy heat. Black inside and out in California."

"It can get surprisingly chilly around here," he said. "Plus, black cars are cool."

Scarlett laughed and slid into the seat. She had to admit that Luke's car offered more legroom than her Prius, not that she intended to mention it. She was loyal to her trusty car.

The Harbor View Inn was a bed-and-breakfast in an old Spanish colonial-style house. The building featured the expected tile roof and a charming arched entrance with ornate tile surrounding the door. But the thick walls were white brick instead of the stucco used on so many buildings of that style.

Scarlett had passed the inn a number of times since it was so close to the museum, but she'd never been inside. The floors were a gorgeous russet tile, and the walls were the same weathered white as the exterior. More arches framed every doorway Scarlett could see. She peeked through one and saw a cozy sitting room full of overstuffed leather furniture set in a conversation-friendly circle.

"This place is beautiful," she said to Luke.

"Thank you," a voice said from the opposite archway. "Welcome to the Harbor View Inn. Do you have a reservation?"

Scarlett and Luke turned.

The woman beaming at them had black hair shot with gray strands, and her eyes were edged by lines. "Oh, I didn't realize it was you, Luke," she said with a smile. "Surely you don't need a room."

"No, I'm actually here to speak to one of your guests," he said.

The warm welcome faded from the woman's face. "Officially?"

"Semiofficially. But nothing too serious." Luke gestured toward Scarlett. "This is Scarlett McCormick. She's the new curator at the museum. Scarlett, this is Mary Gamble, co-owner of the inn."

"How nice to meet you," Mary said, her face wreathed in smiles again. "I've been meaning to get over to the museum since you took over, but this place keeps me so busy. I've seen the advertising about the upcoming mummy exhibit. My husband, Tim, and I are planning to check it out."

Scarlett managed not to wince. She doubted she would have a real mummy to show anyone, but she greeted the woman pleasantly.

"I need to speak with Dr. Sayed Kamal," Luke said. "Is he in?"

Mary frowned for a moment, but she acquiesced. "He's in his room. I saw him go upstairs a few minutes ago. But I must warn you that he's in a foul mood." She huffed. "I'm beginning to suspect that's his default attitude. He's been testing every bit of the patience Tim and I have learned from owning this inn for the last twenty years."

"I'll try not to make things worse," he said.

"Do you need the room number?" Mary asked.

Luke shook his head. "I have it. Thanks. You'd best stay down here so he doesn't associate this visit with you."

"Gladly," Mary said. She directed her welcoming warmth to Scarlett. "Nice meeting you. I hope to see you at the museum soon."

"Thank you. It was nice to meet you too." And that was all Scarlett managed before she had to hurry after Luke.

They climbed the polished wood stairs to Sayed's room. Luke clearly knew his way around the inn, so Scarlett merely trotted after him without comment.

Luke rapped on the mahogany door to the room.

A few moments later, the door opened a crack, and Sayed peered through the narrow gap. "What do you want?"

"I'm Agent Anderson." Luke held up his identification. "I need to speak to you about the artifacts in the collection shipped to Crescent Harbor. Since you were sent to safeguard them, I assume you're conversant with the items shipped."

"Of course I am," Sayed snapped. "But why does an FBI agent want to know?"

"I have my reasons," Luke answered vaguely.

Scarlett leaned around Luke to speak to Sayed. "Do you have the paperwork listing everything that is part of the exhibit? I want to compare your list to the list I made upon opening the crates. I imagine you want to know if anything is missing."

"Missing?" Sayed repeated. "There better not be anything missing. Those items belong to the Egyptian people."

"Not all of them," Scarlett replied. "Mr. Reed said he had purchased some items to add to the Reed Museum collection permanently. Are you saying your list only covers the items that still belong to the Egyptian museum?"

"Fine." Sayed opened the door the slightest bit more, though it still wasn't wide enough to suggest an invitation. "I will come to the museum in the morning and bring you a copy of the list. But I hadn't heard anything about Devon Reed buying antiquities. My list is made up only of items owned by the Egyptian museum."

She nodded. That list would also be useful, because she had no way to know which items were which.

"I assume that once I show you the list, you will be packing up the artifacts for their return to Egypt," Sayed said.

"I haven't decided on that," Scarlett said. "My understanding was that Mr. Reed had an agreement with your employers. That means the museum should still have the right to display them for the agreed time."

"You lost Usewatu," Sayed snapped. "Why should you be allowed to lose anything else?"

"I didn't lose anything," Scarlett protested.

"Hold on," Luke said. "Why don't Scarlett and I come inside so we can discuss this? I'd like to know what you've been doing since you came to Crescent Harbor."

"I will discuss the artifacts at the museum. Tomorrow." With that, Sayed completely ignored the rest of what Luke had said and slammed the door. Scarlett heard the lock engage.

"He doesn't act particularly intimidated by you," Scarlett said.

"Yes, I noticed." Luke studied the door with a frown. "Nothing suspicious there."

15

As Scarlett arrived at the museum on Monday morning, she was relieved to see that most of the reporters were gone. She'd been worried that the reopening would give them an opportunity to make a nuisance of themselves, but apparently the majority had moved on to whatever news story had come out of the bigger cities. She couldn't guess which one. As usual, Scarlett was focused more on her work than the news.

She slipped her Prius into her parking spot and sat there for a moment, basking in the fact that the museum would be taking the first step back to normalcy. Of course, she still had a lot to do. She was determined to sort out the records on the artifacts in the basement, including who owned them and where they'd originated. She also needed to make a final determination on the new exhibit. Would she simply exhibit a closed mummy case, or would she dip into the skills of the Greek to Me Playhouse and make her own mummy? "I'll work it out," she told herself.

When Scarlett entered the museum, she headed straight to Burial Grounds. She could use a cup of coffee, and she wanted to catch Allie up on the rest of her Sunday events.

As usual, her friend greeted her warmly. "Coffee?" Allie asked.

"Yes, please."

Allie began preparing the coffee. "Winnie's here," she said over her shoulder. "I made her a cup of herbal tea this morning. The doctor told her no coffee for a few days after her conk on the head."

"Is she still pale?" Scarlett asked.

Allie reached across the counter and handed Scarlett the cup. "No. She looked and acted completely normal. Well, maybe a little more briskly efficient than usual. I think she's embarrassed about being knocked out, so she's trying to prove that she feels well enough to be at work."

"I got the same impression." Scarlett took a sip of the rich coffee and sighed. "Excellent coffee as always. Did you get some surfing in yesterday?"

"It was magnificent," Allie gushed, then launched into a detailed account of her afternoon of surfing.

Even though it was all English, Scarlett couldn't necessarily understand it. But it didn't matter. She simply sipped her coffee and basked in the ordinary moment.

When Allie finished, she eyed Scarlett. "How much of that did you get?"

"I got the part about how you had a glorious time," Scarlett replied with a smile.

Allie laughed. "That was the gist. Tell me about your Sunday afternoon. Did you spend it with a cat in your lap and your feet up?"

"I spent most of it with Luke," Scarlett replied. "He tracked down Dr. Sayed Kamal at the Harbor View Inn. He wasn't willing to talk to us, but he promised to come to the museum today with a list of the artifacts on loan. That should help me work out some of the background on them."

For a moment, sadness swept over Allie's face. "Did Luke say how close they are to finding Devon's murderer?"

"I'm sorry, but no," Scarlett said gently. "I don't know how involved he is with that case, since it seems to be under the jurisdiction of the local force."

"I wish all that was settled," Allie said. "We haven't even found out anything about a funeral. I have to assume Devon made arrangements in his will. He was a planner that way."

"Have you heard anything about his will?"

Allie shook her head. "Nor have I heard from Peter. He'd know about the will, or maybe the new assistant would. What was her name? Beatrice?"

"Beatrix Morrow," Scarlett said. "I thought we'd see her again, but I suppose she doesn't need to keep doing her job anymore."

"If you hear from her or Peter, please ask about Devon's funeral arrangements," Allie said. "And if it's Peter you hear from, tell him to call me."

"I will," Scarlett promised.

"Good." Allie leaned against the counter. "So, I assume your Sunday afternoon was improved by the addition of the handsome Luke Anderson."

"Luke was working." Scarlett shook a finger at her friend. "No more of that."

"No more of what?" Allie asked innocently. "Work?" She grinned. "Honestly, you can't tell me you didn't notice that Luke is gorgeous."

Of course I noticed. "I'm not having this conversation about a professional colleague," Scarlett said, putting her nose in the air. "I'd best get to my office. I have a ton of work to do." She spun on her heel and marched from the coffee shop with Allie's laughter following her out.

As Scarlett strode through the museum, she noticed people scurrying to get ready for the doors to open at nine. Scarlett pulled her phone from her suit jacket pocket and saw that she had about ten minutes, so she picked up her pace, preferring to be in her office before guests rushed inside full of questions about the events of the last few days.

She was glad to find her office empty and in order when she unlocked the door and walked in. That wasn't a guarantee anymore with the recent break-ins. She settled into her chair and started up her computer to check the museum's email. While she sipped her coffee, she swept through the emails that offered to sell her things vitally necessary for every busy professional and flagged the few remaining messages that actually required her attention and response.

Scarlett had answered about half the emails when she heard a polite knock at her door. "Come in," she sang out.

The door opened, and Sayed entered.

She was surprised that he hadn't barged in.

He held up a leather case. "I have the list of artifacts." His tone didn't sound harsh, a further surprise to Scarlett.

She rose. "Wonderful. Please have a seat and let's go over it."

Sayed accepted her invitation without comment, his movements crisp but not hostile. He sat stiffly in the chair across from Scarlett's desk, withdrew a folder from his case, and gave it to her. "You'll find the list includes information on the point of origin of each artifact."

Scarlett scanned the list. It did indeed include the point of origin, though she saw it didn't mention when each item had entered the Egyptian museum's collection. She brought that up. "I would have liked to put that information on the displays."

He waved away the comment. "Not important."

She raised an eyebrow at the curt dismissal, but she realized it might be possible to get the information she wanted through Winnie's contact at the Egyptian museum, so she didn't push.

Scarlett brought out the list she'd made of every item presently in the basement storage of the museum and started comparing the two lists. For the most part, it was easy. She had extensive working knowledge of Egyptian artifacts, so her guesses of the period of each piece she'd pulled from the crates were proven true over and over. Then she came to a shocking discovery. *Every* item in the museum's basement was also on Sayed's list.

"This list you've given me," Scarlett said, choosing her words carefully. "Every item on it belongs to the Egyptian museum?"

"Yes," he said.

"But this is every item from the storeroom," she said. "Mr. Reed told me some of the collection he was shipping belonged to him, not the museum."

"That is not my problem," Sayed said. "Perhaps he lied. Or the items he owned himself were stolen when he was killed. I do not know. I only know the items on that list belong to Egypt."

"I'll need to authenticate this list," Scarlett said.

His careful veneer of cooperation fell away completely. "The items on that list belong to Egypt." He pounded a fist on her desk. "You will hand them over immediately so they can be returned to my country at once. Considering the impossibly poor security you've provided, the contract is void."

"I will contact the museum's lawyer to see where we stand on that," she said, refusing to allow her own voice to rise in response to his anger. "In addition, I will research each item to be certain that your assertion of ownership is correct unless you can show me more proof than a list you could have made on any computer."

Sayed jumped to his feet. "I will not be insulted this way."

Scarlett got up more slowly. "I will not be intimidated," she said, keeping her tone as reasonable as she could. "I will return the items that belong to the Egyptian museum as soon as I am certain of the authenticity of this list and your claim that we have somehow broken the contract."

"You will not stand in my way based on the lies of a wealthy American," he growled. "A man who clearly thought the cultural artifacts from another country were his for the taking."

"I will do what is required of my job," she said, then gritted her teeth. "Thank you for providing this paperwork. I will begin my authentication immediately, so I would appreciate it if you would leave my office and my museum. Now."

"Leave?" Sayed demanded, almost hoarse with anger. "I will not be leaving our artifacts unguarded around people clearly intent on theft."

Scarlett was glad a desk separated her from the man as his face grew ominously dark with the stress of fury. She cast about for a possible weapon in case Sayed launched himself at her. Her gaze settled on a large round glass paperweight, and she readied herself to grab it if necessary.

The office door opened, and Winnie marched inside, followed by two reassuringly burly security guards. "Are you all right?" she asked Scarlett.

"I'm unharmed," Scarlett said. "Dr. Kamal is leaving the museum now."

"I am not," he protested.

"You are," Winnie assured him. "But you have a choice. You can leave with your dignity intact, or I can have my security guards haul you out and deposit you on the sidewalk in front of the remaining reporters. If you don't want your employers to see photos of you being dragged out of the museum, you will choose the dignified exit."

Sayed glared at Winnie. "Fine. I will leave, but everyone in this room will regret how I have been treated. You will regret it painfully."

The security guards advanced toward him.

Sayed scurried out of the office before they could touch him.

The guards glanced at Winnie.

"Yes," Winnie said. "Please follow Dr. Kamal and make sure he finds his way outside."

With murmured agreement, the men left.

"Are you sure you're all right?" Winnie asked Scarlett.

"I'm annoyed but fine," Scarlett said. She waved the papers at Winnie. "Sayed is claiming that every item in our storeroom belongs to Egypt, which flies directly in the face of what Devon told me. He said some of the pieces would become a permanent part of our collection."

"How did Sayed explain that?" Winnie asked.

"He claimed Devon lied about it," Scarlett said. "Or the items were stolen at the time of the murder."

"That's possible," Winnie said. "Not the liar part. Devon was one of the most honest people I ever met. But maybe his death *was* to cover up a robbery."

"Or Sayed is lying, which is also possible," Scarlett said. "I suppose the pieces Devon bought could still arrive, though I can't imagine why he would have shipped them separately." She sighed deeply and studied the papers on the desk. "I need to track down each and every piece and learn who actually owns it now. This list should help. At least it will give me a starting point."

"If you need any help with that, or anything else, let me know."

"I could probably use the contact information for your source with the Egyptian museum," Scarlett said.

"I'll text the information to you when I get back to my office." Winnie walked to the door. "For now, I should check on my guards and Sayed's present status."

"Thank you for the save—and everything else."

"Always happy to do my job."

After Winnie left, Scarlett slumped into her chair. She had expected her interaction with Sayed to be unpleasant, but it had surpassed even her bleak imagination. With each encounter, she felt more convinced that Devon's death was somehow linked to the artifacts.

For now, the most important thing she could do was track down each item's actual ownership. If the list Sayed had given her included items the Egyptian museum didn't own, it would suggest Sayed could be Devon's killer. The police suspected him, but they couldn't do much without proof.

Scarlett felt a chill as the next logical bit of the puzzle fell into place in her head. If Sayed was the killer, then he might not be done killing, not when his plan could still be thwarted. That meant if proof did exist, she needed to find it fast before anything happened to prevent that.

Permanently.

16

Scarlett raised her arms to stretch, attempting to pull the kinks out of her spine. The museum was closed, but she had stuck with her task of researching the artifacts on her list.

She was absolutely certain that every item in the basement storeroom was on Sayed's list, and she had tracked a few of the pieces to the collection of the Egyptian museum. The search was helped along by the call to Winnie's contact at the museum, but he had admitted that he wasn't as knowledgeable about the list as Sayed. Scarlett had gotten the impression that admission was grudging. Even a brief conversation made it clear the man despised Sayed Kamal.

Scarlett knew that professional rivalries in academic circles could be vicious, so the man's feelings didn't prove anything. Sayed could be incredibly good at his job and still be obnoxious. The two weren't mutually exclusive.

For that reason, it was desperation that pushed Scarlett to call Professor Victor Aigner. She had to search for the phone number, but she recognized the stentorian voice of the professor the moment he answered the phone.

"This is Scarlett McCormick with the Reed Museum of Art and Archaeology in Crescent Harbor, California. I was hoping you have a moment to assist me."

"Is this the Scarlett McCormick who took my graduate course in Egyptian history?" the professor asked.

She suppressed a groan. She'd rather hoped to speak to the man based on her present credentials, not on discussions they'd had when she was in his class. Professor Aigner had not been Scarlett's biggest fan. He had a rather narrow view about women in archaeology, and she doubted she'd helped him change, but he was also one of the premier experts on Egyptian antiquities. "Yes, though my present difficulty lies with the museum, not my studies."

"Probably for the best," he said.

Scarlett gritted her teeth. She'd earned an A in that class, and it hadn't come easy.

"What can I do for you?"

Scarlett tapped her fingers against her desk, hoping to work off some of her nervous energy and keep it out of her voice. She explained the situation at the museum, the artifacts, and the problems with authenticating and tracing the ownership of each piece without the proper papers.

Professor Aigner never interrupted her. When she finished, he simply asked, "What have you done so far?"

She told him and waited for him to say how completely inadequate her efforts had been. *Why did I think I should call this man?* "I have exhausted most of my connections, save a few who are unreachable on account of being scattered across the globe at various digs. But I hoped you'd have some suggestions for my next step."

For a long moment, the professor gave no answer. "I realize I gave you a difficult time in the class you took with me. I felt that you were a student who responded well to challenge. And you did, bringing serious academic rigor to your work. You've shown that again here."

Scarlett held the phone in a shaking hand, her mind reeling. Was Professor Aigner giving her a compliment? "Thank you, sir."

He ignored the thanks and pressed on. "As you've clearly learned, the ownership of Egyptian artifacts remains a touchy business. Some private collectors prefer to keep their collections quiet to avoid the censure of cultural appropriation. This makes them reluctant to speak with anyone they do not know."

She sighed. "So I can expect to run into more walls."

"Perhaps I can help," the professor offered. "Email me the list, and I promise to see what I can do to track down who presently owns them. As it happens, I *am* someone most of the private collectors know. I should have some useful information for you by tomorrow."

"That would be wonderful," Scarlett said. "Thank you, sir."

"It is my pleasure to be of assistance," he said. He rattled off his email address, saying it only once before wishing her a good night and ending the call.

She opened her email and added the professor to her contacts while his address was fresh in her head. Then she wrote an email, cutting and pasting the list of artifacts and adding everything she'd been able to learn. She ended the email with more thanks before sending it.

The phone rang, startling her. She rarely received calls so long after closing time.

When she picked up the phone, someone whispered, "Scarlett McCormick?"

For an instant, Scarlett responded to the whisper with alarm, but then she recognized it as Officer Nina Garcia. "How can I help you?"

"Actually, I think I can help you," Garcia said, her voice still unusually quiet. "Do you know Peter Vore?"

"I've met him once. I know he's in town."

"He's been badgering the chief to arrest you," the officer said.

"Me?" Scarlett asked, stunned.

"Peter says you're the only change at the museum," Garcia responded. "He knows and trusts everyone else, so he assumes you must be the murderer. The chief isn't giving it a lot of credence, but I wanted to alert you that someone is blaming you for Devon Reed's murder."

"Thank you for telling me," Scarlett said.

"Don't mention it to the chief," the officer whispered. "I expect he would be mad, but I felt it was something you should know, so you can be careful around Peter, if nothing else."

"I won't breathe a word to Chief Rodriguez," Scarlett said. "I appreciate the warning."

Garcia gasped and ended the call.

Scarlett stared at the phone, worried. She hoped Garcia hadn't been caught making a call she shouldn't. She hated to think the officer would get into trouble for cautioning her about Devon's former assistant.

That led her to the next annoyance. Why exactly was Peter Vore blaming her for murder? She supposed his reasoning made a certain vague sense. If he trusted everyone else, then the newcomer was the best suspect, but Scarlett still thought the accusation was ridiculous. Thankfully, Garcia had suggested the chief felt the same way.

"No point fretting about it now," Scarlett said aloud as she stood and began gathering her papers. She considered dumping them in the lockable drawer in her desk, but a nagging worry made her decide to put them somewhere a bit more secure. She carried them to the small safe in the office. She suspected she was being overly cautious, but she'd rest easier if she knew the information would be safely waiting for her in the morning.

She'd just closed the safe when she heard a rap at the office door.

"Come in," Scarlett called.

Winnie entered with Beatrix Morrow in tow. Scarlett realized that she'd nearly forgotten about Devon's young assistant, especially with Devon's previous assistant making so much trouble.

"Miss Morrow wanted to speak to you," Winnie said. "If you don't need me, I should adjust the night shift security schedule before the shift change actually happens."

"No problem," Scarlett said. "Thank you. Please don't overdo it."

"I won't," Winnie promised.

Since she appeared fine, Scarlett didn't argue.

Winnie backed out of the office and closed the door.

Scarlett offered what she hoped was a warm greeting to Beatrix. "What can you tell me about the artifacts for the exhibit? I need to know which of them belong to the Egyptian museum and which of them belonged directly to Devon Reed."

The young woman blinked at her. "I wasn't involved with that. I mostly buy Devon's plane tickets and make sure he doesn't forget meetings. Didn't all the artifacts belong to the Egyptian museum? Devon told me he was borrowing a huge number of things for the exhibit. He wanted it to go well since it was going to be the first big event you'd be handling."

"Devon told me that he was also including artifacts that he owned," Scarlett said, trying to keep her tone patient.

"Oh, he never said anything like that to me," Beatrix said. "In fact, I remember there was one pot that he specifically said he wished he owned." She shrugged. "Maybe he had more items in storage? I'm not sure. I was his personal assistant, and he was aware that I didn't know anything about art and antiquities."

"But he apparently spoke to you a little about the exhibit," Scarlett reasoned.

"Yes, Devon talked about it," Beatrix said. "He loved to discuss artifacts. He could spend hours talking about the type of glaze used on different types of pottery. I often drifted when he launched into art talk. If I didn't need to schedule it or file it away, I tended to tune it out."

Scarlett thought that was a terrible thing for an assistant to do, but Devon hadn't struck her as a man who accepted shoddy work, so Beatrix must have been competent. Besides, there was no reason for Scarlett to scold the young woman for a job she no longer had. There was another topic she wanted to discuss. "Were you aware that Peter Vore is here in Crescent Harbor?"

Beatrix's shocked expression made it clear she didn't know. "Why?"

"Apparently, he wants to know who killed Devon," Scarlett said. "I've been told they were close."

"I think they were at some point," Beatrix said, "but I also think that changed."

"What makes you say that?"

"I never met Peter personally," Beatrix answered. "Sometimes Devon mentioned him, and he sounded funny every time. At first, I thought he was annoyed at losing an assistant he'd worked with for so long, but the more I heard it, the more I started to wonder. I think Devon was scared of him."

Scarlett raised her eyebrows. "You think Devon was afraid of his previous assistant?"

"Not terrified or anything," Beatrix said swiftly. "Maybe more concerned. I did see something in the financial record that was kind of weird."

"What was it?"

"Devon gave Peter a lot of money when he left the job," Beatrix said. "Way too much to be severance pay, unless Devon paid the guy ten times what he pays me."

"Did you ever ask Devon about it?"

Beatrix widened her eyes. "Of course not. It wasn't my business, and I expect he'd have bitten my head off. I told you because you asked about it. Do you think I should tell the police?"

"Probably," Scarlett said. She thought about Peter's anger when she'd met him and now the fact that he was trying to blame Scarlett for Devon's death. Was it possible that the man was trying to deflect attention from himself? Maybe he jumped in with an accusation before suspicion could settle on him.

"There's one other thing," Beatrix said, dropping her voice as if concerned about being overheard in the private office.

"What's that?"

"I didn't do the artifact stuff," Beatrix reminded her. "But I did keep up with his personal paperwork. I've seen his will. Devon was constantly updating it, and every time he did, I had to file a copy. Anyway, I know he left small sums of money to tons of people he knew, even some former employees—but nothing for Peter. I figure that might say something about how Devon felt about him."

"Maybe," Scarlett said, though she wasn't convinced. If Devon had already given Peter a large amount of money, he could simply feel he'd been generous enough. Nothing Beatrix was saying was proof of anything. However, it *was* interesting.

A question flitted through Scarlett's head. "I never asked what brought you here today. Is there anything I can help you with?"

"Actually, it's about the will," Beatrix said. "There's something you should be aware of, so you don't get blindsided when it's read."

"Blindsided by what?" Scarlett asked.

"As I said, Devon left money to lots of people and even a few organizations, mainly colleges. He enjoyed assisting people who wanted to better themselves, and he said college kids needed help these days."

"I don't doubt that," Scarlett agreed, mostly to move the young woman's disclosure along. What could any of this have to do with Scarlett?

"Anyway, I noticed one thing that surprised me," Beatrix said. "This museum isn't mentioned in the will. I thought you should know, since I figure a place like this must be expensive. Actually, I know it is because I've seen some of the expenditure reports. I filed them."

Scarlett sat motionless, trying to process what the woman had said. Devon Reed had left nothing to the museum he'd founded? That made no sense. How could she possibly keep the museum open with no more financial help?

She felt a surge of panic. This could be the end of everything.

17

Beatrix peered at Scarlett, her expression filled with sympathy. "I'm so sorry," she whispered.

"Why wouldn't Devon mention the museum in his will?" Scarlett asked, speaking as much to herself as Beatrix. Every person she'd spoken with since taking the curator job agreed on one thing: Devon Reed loved the museum.

"I don't know," Beatrix said. "He didn't discuss it with me. I only saw it because I handled it after the fact. To be honest, Devon was an eccentric man. He changed his mind frequently and radically in the time I worked for him."

Her words penetrated the haze. "Are you suggesting he was mentally unwell?"

Beatrix shook her head, sending her curls swinging. "No, not at all. He was eccentric and sometimes unpredictable, but I don't think he was disturbed or anything." She sounded flustered. "Maybe I shouldn't have said anything. I should go. You have a lot to do."

"Thanks for telling me," Scarlett said.

Beatrix didn't say anything else. She slipped out of the office, leaving the door open behind her.

Scarlett wondered if she was earning Beatrix's "eccentric" label herself. She felt that the last week had left her a bit wobbly.

Winnie poked her head in the office. "I sent one of my people to help Beatrix find her way out." The head of security leaned in a little more, studying Scarlett. "Are you okay?"

"I'm flummoxed," Scarlett admitted. "Beatrix said she's seen Devon's will. The museum isn't in it."

Winnie marched into the room and sat down across from Scarlett's desk. "That makes no sense."

"I thought the same."

Winnie continued as if Scarlett hadn't spoken. "Devon told me more than once that this museum was one of his favorite places, somewhere he always felt as if he belonged. He thought the museum was his way of giving something lasting to the community and ensuring the past was made real for people."

Scarlett listened to Winnie voice the exact same things Devon had told her. It was hard to believe that he'd left the museum out of his will. "Maybe he made some other arrangements. Something outside the will."

"I guess that's possible," Winnie said, her voice unusually hesitant. "I'm no lawyer. But I know one thing without a doubt. Devon didn't turn his back on this museum."

"I hope not," Scarlett said. "But it would help explain why he hadn't been coming to visit very often anymore. Perhaps he had lost interest in it."

"No, that would never happen," Winnie insisted.

Scarlett hadn't known the man well enough to argue the point. "It would be best if I begin researching possible fundraising plans. If Devon didn't provide for the museum, we're going to have a lot of work ahead of us to keep it open."

Winnie sniffed. "I don't mean to place blame, but Beatrix strikes me as a bit scatterbrained. She may be wrong. Maybe she saw a different document and was confused. Or maybe she made up the whole thing to appear important."

"Why would she care about whether or not I think she's important?" Scarlett asked.

Winnie barked a single laugh. "You're a formidable person. She probably admires you. Who knows?"

"I should speak to her again," Scarlett said. Then she smacked her forehead. "I should have thought to ask her where she's staying."

Winnie grinned. "Do you really think I'd let her up here without knowing how to track her down? Beatrix Morrow has a room at the Harbor View Inn."

Scarlett leaned forward. "That's the same place Sayed is staying."

"It could simply be a coincidence," Winnie suggested. "After all, the inn is close to the museum."

"You're probably right." But Scarlett wasn't sure. At the moment, she found herself suspicious of all the new people she'd met in the past week. And that led her to another potential suspect. "Do you know Peter Vore?"

"I've met him," Winnie said. "He seemed like a nice guy. Allie knows him a lot better."

"He's in town. Apparently, he's been pressuring the police to consider me a suspect in Devon's murder." Scarlett thought about telling Winnie that the man had even come to her house, she but discarded the idea immediately. Winnie might insist on camping out there to keep her safe.

"You?" Winnie asked. "Why you?"

"He said it's because he trusts everyone else at the museum," Scarlett answered. "I'd like to ask him about that, and I plan to if I can. I wonder what the odds are that Peter is booked at the Harbor View Inn as well."

"I could find out," Winnie offered. "I've known the owners for a while, though Luke knows Tim and Mary Gamble much better. If I can't get them to tell me, I'll guarantee Luke can. His way with people is impressive."

"I want to see inside Peter's room wherever he's staying," Scarlett said. "I also want to see Beatrix's room. Maybe throw Sayed's room in there as well. Someone has more information about Devon and why he was killed."

"We couldn't get into the rooms legally without an invitation," Winnie said. "Technically, if they're all staying at the Harbor View Inn, Mary could get into the rooms anytime she needs access."

"Do you think she'd let us in?" Scarlett asked. "Or barring that, do you think she'd search the rooms for evidence?"

Winnie wrinkled her nose. "No, I think not. Mary wouldn't want anyone at her inn breaking the law, and she wouldn't want to aid a murderer or inhibit the hunt for a murderer. But I think she'd have to see some serious proof that we had good cause to suspect one of her guests. And we don't. We're basically fishing here."

"I guess we'll have to scrap that idea," Scarlett said glumly.

"For now," Winnie said. "But if I poke into Beatrix's background, things could change."

"While you're doing that, I want to know more about Peter," Scarlett said. "I think he's acting questionably, and Beatrix said Devon gave him a large amount of money when Peter left his employ. I need to know if that's true, because I find it suspicious."

"I'll check into that too," Winnie said. "Devon was a generous man, so if he and Peter parted ways on good terms—and I'd be shocked if they didn't—I could see Devon giving him money."

"Within reason," Scarlett said. "At this point, we don't know exactly how much the sum of money was. If it was big enough, I'd consider it worth investigating further."

Winnie nodded. "I'm on it."

"Thanks." Scarlett remembered Winnie's recent injury, so she added, "Don't worry about it right now. Tomorrow is soon enough.

We've both worked enough hours today. And one of us needs to go home, put her feet up, and continue to recover from a head injury."

"I'm fine, but I'm happy to go home." Winnie stood. "Good night."

"See you tomorrow." Scarlett waved Winnie out the door.

While Scarlett prepared for her own departure, she was relieved that no one else showed up at her office. She'd had enough surprises for one day. She planned to follow much of the advice she'd given Winnie. She'd go home, put her feet up, and fuss over Cleo.

As she switched off the light to the office, her thoughts turned to how well Winnie was recovering from her injury, then to the other person she'd seen lately who wasn't doing so well. She wondered how Hershel was feeling.

The retired curator had been so sweet to her, and he'd talked to Devon much more than she had. He might know if Devon had a long-term plan for funding the museum, something outside a mention in his will. Scarlett pondered whether it was fair to ask the ailing man questions that could possibly upset him.

By the time she'd argued back and forth for a while, she was outside and halfway to her car. At that point, she decided on a compromise. She'd drive to Hershel's house and see how he was doing. If he seemed up to it, she would consider asking him. But if he was weaker, she'd find the information she needed some other way.

With that decision made, Scarlett hopped in the car, feeling better. She'd always preferred facing a problem and doing something about it. Indecision wasn't normally part of her personality.

When she reached his home, she noticed there were no lights on inside. The afternoon sun was fading, and it must have been getting dark inside the house.

Scarlett hurried to the door, her stomach knotting slightly in worry. Hershel might be taking a nap. Still, too many troublesome things had happened in the last week, and she was eager to discover the elderly man was fine.

She knocked on the door and waited with all the patience she could muster. She knew Hershel wouldn't be able to move quickly. When she couldn't wait any longer, she knocked again, striking the door hard enough to make her knuckles ache.

The knock had no result—no sounds from inside, no response whatsoever.

Scarlett rationalized that Hershel might be out with his grandson. It was reasonable, but she couldn't quite force herself to return to her car. Instead, she studied the front of the house, trying to determine which windows would look in on the sitting room where she'd chatted with Hershel on the last visit.

She slipped behind a low hedge to peer into the window, hoping no neighbor spotted her skulking around and called the police. *I'm not nosy. I'm not intrusive. I'm concerned.*

Most of the view through the glass was blocked by the dark curtains, but a gap near the bottom revealed the room inside was dim and shadowy. Scarlett stretched on her toes for the right angle and saw a mound on the floor. She pressed her face still closer to the glass.

It was Hershel, and he wasn't moving.

18

Scarlett rapped on the glass several times, then backed away from the window and pulled out her phone to call for help. She explained exactly what she'd seen to the operator. As she talked, she returned to the front door to check if it was unlocked so she could render aid to Hershel while she waited for the ambulance. The door was locked. Scarlett circled the house, trying windows and doors. Finally, at the rear of the house, she found an unlocked window. She pushed it up and crawled inside.

She tumbled gracelessly into a laundry room and raced through the house to the sitting room. Hershel hadn't moved at all. She dropped to her knees, nearly weeping with fear, and pressed her fingers against the side of his neck.

With a sob of relief, she felt the throb of a pulse. Hershel was alive.

Since Hershel was already in a basic rescue position, Scarlett didn't try to move him. She simply covered him with the afghan that was draped over the back of the sofa and spoke to him quietly, assuring him that help was coming. There was no sign that the unconscious man heard her, but she felt better for having said the words.

Scarlett was still holding the elderly man's hand when she heard sirens. "They're here," she told Hershel in a cheery voice. "You're going to be fine." She gently returned his hand to his chest and rushed to the door to let the emergency crew in.

As soon as they entered the house, Scarlett was rendered superfluous. Two paramedics knelt down beside Hershel and started examining him. They knew their job so well that simply seeing them work with such brisk efficiency made Scarlett finally feel the hope she'd been trying to convey to the unconscious man.

Officer James Young approached Scarlett. His intelligent blue eyes were wryly amused. "Can you tell me how you happened to be in the victim's home, keeping in mind that you had to unlock the door to let us in?"

"Hershel Smythe," she said almost automatically. She hated to hear the stricken man referred to as "the victim."

Officer Young tipped his head at the mild rebuke built into the reminder, but he didn't speak, clearly waiting for her explanation.

"He didn't answer the door, and it concerned me," Scarlett said. "When I'd met him the other day, he clearly wasn't well."

The officer pursed his lips, still refraining from comment.

"I'll admit to peeking through the window," she continued. "I saw him on the floor in the sitting room, and I called 911."

He nodded.

"I considered waiting outside," Scarlett said. "But if there was something I could do to help while I waited and I didn't do it, I couldn't bear it. I found an unlocked window to the laundry room and climbed into the house." She tried to make the whole speech without sounding guilty and apologetic, but she faded a bit at the end.

"What aid did you render?"

"I covered him with the afghan and held his hand," Scarlett replied, knowing it sounded weak.

"I think you did the right thing," Officer Young said, "and I believe Mr. Smythe will agree. I doubt you'll make a habit of breaking and entering. Don't worry. I'd say calling for help may easily have saved Mr. Smythe's life."

She glanced at the unconscious man and whispered, "I hope so."

Tuesday morning dawned with more of the beautiful California weather Scarlett had come to expect, even in September. She'd fretted about Hershel for most of the previous evening, causing Cleo to become grumpy at her distraction. Scarlett's worry had chased her into her dreams, leaving her feeling groggy when the alarm went off, despite the cheerful morning sun dancing on her white duvet.

As Scarlett prepared to head to the museum, she did her makeup and chose her outfit with special care, striving for a combination that would lessen the visible results of a poor night's sleep. She paired a blue sleeveless blouse with an unlined blazer in charcoal gray. The blue matched the lovely sunny day, and the charcoal suited her mood. She might not feel refreshed, but she would be content if she came across as competent and professional.

By the time she reached the museum, she was nearly desperate for a cup of coffee. The one she'd gulped down at home had barely made a dent in her mood.

As usual, Allie greeted her with appalling bright-eyed cheerfulness. "Good morning," her friend sang out. "It's an ideal day for surfing."

"You think every day is ideal for surfing," Scarlett grumbled as she leaned on the counter. She would have liked to put her head down, but that would be defeatist.

"Because it is." Allie set about making Scarlett's coffee without being asked. "You sound out of sorts."

"I didn't sleep well," Scarlett said. "Hershel Smythe is in the hospital."

Allie froze. "That's terrible. Is he going to be okay?"

"I don't know. I found him unconscious on the floor at his house yesterday. I have no idea how long he'd been that way."

Allie put the cup of coffee in front of Scarlett and patted her arm.

"I assume you were the one to call the ambulance."

Scarlett nodded and sipped the coffee. "I also called the hospital last night, but they refused to tell me anything because I'm not family. I'm planning to stop by after work."

"I should too. Hershel is such a sweetie."

Scarlett wasn't sure she would have described the rather formal gentleman that way, but she agreed with the overall sentiment.

"Speaking of sweeties," Allie said, "Peter came by my house last night."

That perked up all of Scarlett's senses, wiping the grogginess away as if she'd gulped down the coffee instead of simply sipped it. "I assume you let him in."

Allie rolled her eyes. "Of course. I've known Peter for years. I told you I dated him for a while. I'm hardly going to make him stand outside in the dark."

"People can change."

"Not that much." Allie laughed. "I must say, he trusts you about as much as you trust him. For two people who don't know each other, you both have been eager to jump to conclusions."

"And his conclusion is that I killed Devon."

"I told him that's ridiculous," Allie said. "I think he's softening."

"Do you know why he quit working for Devon?" Scarlett asked.

"He got married," Allie said. "He showed me his wife's picture. Sofia is adorable. They're going to have gorgeous kids."

"He quit a good job because he got married?" Scarlett let her incredulity ring in her voice. "I would think a man would want to hold on to a job if he was starting a family."

"He has a job at a large European company with an office in Italy, where he lives now," Allie said. "He switched because he wanted a job that didn't send him all over the world. He thinks Sofia deserves to actually see him every day."

"Did you learn anything about the money Devon gave him?"

"Peter volunteered the information. Devon gave him a wedding gift of enough money to buy a big home in Italy since they're planning to have kids. And that doesn't surprise me. Devon was generous that way." Allie leaned on the counter. "It was exactly the sort of story I expected to hear. Every time I talked to Devon, he sang Peter's praises. I knew he'd never simply decide to replace him."

"I don't suppose Peter said anything to you about the new assistant, did he?" Scarlett asked. "Beatrix Morrow?"

"I did ask," Allie said proudly. "I'm so good at this investigating stuff. Peter said he didn't really know her, but she must excel at the job. Devon was always a great judge of character."

"Since you're so good at investigating," Scarlett said with a smile, "did you happen to ask him if he'd ever crossed paths with Sayed when he worked for Devon?"

Allie positively beamed. "Yes, I did."

"And what did he say?" Scarlett prompted.

"He said he hadn't," Allie replied. "But he insisted that's not unusual. Staff changes often at museums."

Scarlett knew that was true, so she had nothing else to ask. She wasn't completely sure she was ready to eliminate Peter as a possible suspect. All the things he'd said to Allie sounded good, but that didn't mean they were true, nor that there was nothing else going on. But she wasn't going to convince Allie to be suspicious of her friend.

Scarlett held up the cup of coffee and said, "Thanks for the excellent coffee and investigative work."

"Anytime," Allie said.

Scarlett carried the coffee out of Burial Grounds, sipping as she walked. The lobby of the museum was empty, since they were still an hour away from opening. She gazed down the long open space dotted with contemporary sculptures, mostly on historical themes, though with the more abstract pieces it could be hard to tell. In the distance, she spotted Hal and Greta with their heads together, probably discussing the day's docent duties.

Greta turned her head and noticed Scarlett. She raised a hand to wave, and Scarlett returned the friendly gesture. Scarlett had to admit the welcome she'd gotten at the museum was one of the warmest she'd received anywhere she'd worked. She was beginning to see Crescent Harbor and the Reed Museum as a place to settle rather than a stepping stone on her adventure.

Assuming the museum stays open. Her concerns about the will flooded into her mind, and she thought about ducking back into the coffee shop to discuss them with Allie. Scarlett shook off the idea. Allie didn't need to carry her worries.

Squaring her shoulders, Scarlett headed for the stairs and the floor above where her continued search for answers about the new artifacts waited.

As she settled in at her desk with her half-empty coffee, the phone rang. To Scarlett's delight, it was a return call from Professor Victor Aigner, and he had news.

"I haven't completed tracking down the artifacts," the professor said, his voice slipping into the tone he often used when he thought students were rushing ahead too quickly. "But I did find something I knew you would want to know."

"Which is?" Scarlett asked.

The professor tutted, but he refrained from an outright scolding over her impatience. "I located the owner of the two ushabti figures made from faience. They came from the same collection. Your detailed description of the tin-glazed pottery was helpful. I learned the ownership on the list you gave me was correct but not complete. The collector you listed told me that he sold the two pieces to another collector—a man named Christopher Pinchot in Yorkshire, England."

She remained silent as she jotted down notes.

"As it happens, I know Pinchot, and I was able to call him directly," Professor Aigner continued. "He recognized the pieces immediately from my description. He had purchased them for their well-preserved state and the fact that the figures were so similar but carried different items. One held a hoe and the other a basket. He also believed the figures came from the same burial site."

Although Scarlett had examined the figures only once, she was inclined to agree with that assessment. Ushabti represented servants to assist the deceased in the next life. The fact that the two figures had such strong similarities in style and glazing suggested they were made by the same artisan and probably for the same burial site.

"Did he say why he'd sold the figures to the Egyptian museum?" she asked.

"That's what I thought you would find most interesting," the professor said. "Pinchot didn't sell the figures to the Egyptian museum. He sold them to Devon Reed. And he did so because he was an old friend of the billionaire and he was offered enough money to soften his attachment to the pieces."

Scarlett scribbled more notes. "Those ushabti belonged to Devon."

"Unless Pinchot lied to me, and I see no reason for that," Professor Aigner said. "He knows me, and he's aware it would tarnish his reputation to lie to me."

"Did he give you any details of the sale?" she asked.

"Not on the phone, though Pinchot did say he'd send you copies of the paperwork from the sale if you contacted him. I will share his contact information." The professor paused. "He told me something else you may not know."

"What's that?" Scarlett asked.

"As I mentioned, Pinchot was acquainted with Devon Reed for some time. He said the billionaire had been receiving death threats. Now, death threats are sadly a part of being wealthy, so the situation wasn't exactly new or even surprising. But evidently something about these threats alarmed the billionaire and led to his substantial withdrawal from public life. Reed even began avoiding old friends. I suspect he thought his presence would endanger them."

"Did Mr. Pinchot know what form the threats took?"

"No," Professor Aigner admitted sadly. "I believe Pinchot would have told me if he'd known because he seemed eager to gossip. Though Pinchot is quite wealthy, apparently Reed was several notches above him."

"It would have been nice if Devon had hinted at who was threatening him," she remarked.

"Pinchot has a theory."

"He does?"

The professor's voice reflected real pleasure at the conversation. Scarlett had never suspected the outwardly rather stodgy academic had such a love of gossip. "Yes, Pinchot suspected Peter Vore, Reed's former assistant."

Scarlett stifled a gasp. It was a shock, coming so soon after a conversation with Allie about the same man. "Did he say why?"

"Timing, mostly," the professor said. "The first alarming death threat came before this Vore character left Reed's employ and continued from then on. Pinchot thought what made the death threats scare Reed was something to do with how much the sender knew about Reed's movements and past. And that was information Vore had."

"Did Christopher Pinchot know Peter Vore?"

"No," the professor admitted. "He said he'd never actually met the assistant face-to-face. Since Pinchot and Reed were friendly acquaintances, the billionaire made most of their contacts directly."

"Any other revelations?" she asked.

"Is that not enough?"

"It's enough to leave me stunned," Scarlett said. "And you'll send me Mr. Pinchot's contact information?"

"I will," the professor promised. "Along with the other two collectors I contacted. Their pieces were sold to the Egyptian museum, so they don't conflict with what you already knew."

She pulled her list out of the pile. "Which pieces?"

The professor named one of the soapstone scarab amulets, a handsome reddish earthenware bowl, and a matched pair of canopic jars in glazed composition.

Scarlett was mildly sad about the bowl as it was a lovely piece, but she was less disappointed by the amulet and canopic jars, as there were better examples of both in the Reed Museum's collection.

"Thank you for all the work you've done on this," she said sincerely.

"I'll keep on," the professor offered. "I must be honest. This is the most fun I've had in a long time. I'll update you as soon as I have anything new and interesting to report."

Scarlett thanked him again before they ended the call. She was glad the professor was enjoying the task, especially since he was getting crucial results.

Now she knew for certain that not every piece in those crates downstairs belonged to the Egyptian museum. Which led to one vital question: Why had Sayed insisted they did? Was he simply hoping to take advantage of an unfortunate incident to reclaim artifacts for Egypt? Or had the man actually killed Devon for the purpose of acquiring *all* the artifacts?

The more Scarlett pondered it, the more she couldn't quite accept it. She could see Sayed taking advantage. He clearly felt the Egyptian museum was the rightful owner, no matter what the law said. With his temper, she could even see him killing the billionaire in a fit of rage. But she couldn't picture him risking damage to an Egyptian mummy by hauling it out of the coffin. That didn't line up with what she knew about Sayed's passion for antiquities.

But what if he'd been able to remove the mummy under safe conditions? What if he'd done it before the coffin was ever sent to the ship? Then he might be a more viable murder suspect. Of course, that was dipping deeply into hypotheticals.

That left Scarlett with another big question. Was Peter a good guy or a bad guy? Allie considered him a good guy, and Scarlett was inclined to trust her friend over some stranger she hadn't even spoken to. But Scarlett wouldn't mind discussing the death threats with the former assistant—and possibly clearing her own name with him.

She hopped up and dropped her empty cup into the trash before leaving the office. She was careful to lock the door behind her. She wouldn't risk a repeat of the incident with Winnie. For now, the only time her office would be unlocked would be when she was inside.

When Scarlett reached Burial Grounds, she found several museum patrons queued up for coffee inside the shop. She was slightly surprised to see them. Somehow the last hour had flown by. She lingered at a display of coffee cups with the Burial Grounds logo printed on them and waited for Allie to deal with the waiting customers, proud that she managed not to fidget.

The coffee shop wasn't overly large. Patrons mainly carried their coffee out to one of the benches throughout the huge lobby or into the contemporary sculpture area. The benches offered an opportunity for guests to revel in the sunlight through the windows and the beauty of the sculptures while enjoying their drinks.

Finally, the coffee shop was empty. Scarlett knew that wouldn't last so she practically ran to the counter.

"You look ready to burst," Allie said. "You can't be desperate for another cup of coffee already."

"No, it's conversation I want," Scarlett said. As quickly as she could without losing clarity, she explained what she had learned from Professor Aigner. "Have you ever heard of Christopher Pinchot?"

"No, but that's not a surprise," Allie said. "Devon knew so many people, but when he was in Crescent Harbor, he acted as though we were the only ones who mattered."

Scarlett dreaded asking her friend the next question, but there was no way around it. "Did you know Devon had been getting death threats?"

Allie's face clouded. "No, but I don't think he would have told me about anything like that, since he knew I would be concerned. Years ago, he remarked that being a public figure of any kind brought out anger in some people, and that led to some nasty mail. When I had asked for more details, he told me not to worry about it."

"According to Christopher Pinchot, Devon had begun getting death threats that really scared him."

"How horrible," Allie said.

"The man I spoke to believes Devon was cutting himself off from the people and places he cared about because he didn't want to endanger them. Apparently, these threats were that frightening."

Allie shook her head slowly, clearly struggling to process what Scarlett had told her. "I hadn't spoken to Devon much lately, but I figured he was simply busy. He did that, falling off the radar for long stretches. It was nearly always because he was into something that consumed his attention. Devon threw himself into everything he did."

"Do you think Devon would have told you if he'd been afraid of someone?"

"Unless he thought I was in danger too, I don't think he would have brought it up." Allie sighed. "But if he thought looping me in might put me in danger, I could see him keeping his distance."

"This collector said these specific death threats began shortly before Peter stopped working for Devon," Scarlett said. "Is it possible that your friend would know more about the threats?"

"Maybe," Allie said. "But if they started after Peter was engaged, Devon would have kept him in the dark too. He wouldn't have wanted to do anything to wreck Peter's wedding or new life. And he would have known Peter wouldn't leave if he thought Devon was in danger. I know you and Peter didn't exactly hit it off, but Peter is very loyal."

"So are you," Scarlett said.

Allie frowned. "You can't still suspect Peter. Devon bought him a house, remember? Why would Peter have done anything to harm the man who had been kind to him for years?"

As her friend stood before her with her hands on her hips and her hazel eyes blazing, Scarlett had to admit that she couldn't imagine a single reason.

But that didn't mean there wasn't one.

19

When Scarlett returned to her office, she sat down at her desk and removed her phone from her jacket pocket. She had thought of someone who might help her follow some of the leads she'd discovered: Luke Anderson.

Luke answered immediately. "What can I do for you?"

She shifted papers nervously around her desk as she explained what she'd learned from Professor Aigner. "I think the police need this information. It proves Sayed lied to me, and I know they were considering him a suspect in Devon's murder."

"How can I help?" he asked.

"I suppose I'm hoping for advice," Scarlett responded. "How do I go about sharing this information with the police? I don't want to come across as if I have a vendetta against Sayed, especially since I know Peter Vore told the police he thinks I killed Devon."

"You're well-informed," Luke remarked. "I only recently heard about Peter Vore's accusation. Maybe I should try to recruit you for the FBI."

"No thank you. I prefer being an archaeologist and curator. It means most of the dead people I meet have been that way for a long, long time."

"I can see the appeal," he said. "What you've learned about Sayed makes me curious. He could simply be an opportunist, using the death of Devon to further his agenda."

"Yes, I have considered that." Scarlett returned to shifting papers.

She knew what Luke said was reasonable, but she was seriously short on suspects if she removed Sayed. And if she believed Allie when she said Peter couldn't possibly have killed Devon.

"Or Sayed could be the killer and is unquestionably a liar," Luke said, cutting into her thoughts. "He refused to let us inside his room at the bed-and-breakfast, and that makes me wonder what sort of incriminating evidence he may be hiding. If we found something that proved he was lying to you, it would give the police more leverage in questioning him."

"If Sayed has the original paperwork, that would be a big help," Scarlett said. "We need those artifacts to go to the museum, especially if what Devon's assistant told me is true."

"What's that?" he asked.

Scarlett felt the problem bubble in her chest, so she rushed through her answer. "Devon didn't include the museum in his will. We could be in serious financial trouble."

"That doesn't sound like him."

Scarlett remained silent because she didn't know how to respond. More and more, she was realizing she didn't actually have any idea what Devon Reed had been like.

"We need to take this one step at a time," Luke advised. "Considering the lies swirling around them and the missing mummy, I think the artifacts are the link to more information about Devon's death. I'll call Chief Rodriguez and update you on what he says."

Scarlett thanked him and ended the call. She wasn't sure that the artifacts *were* at the center of everything. Peter had left Devon's employ with enough money to buy a house in Italy long before the artifacts were shipped to Crescent Harbor. Devon had begun receiving death threats around that time, threats unusual enough to alarm the billionaire. *I should have told Luke that.*

She grabbed a piece of paper and started making a list of all the anomalous things. Peter's huge gift from Devon. Was it out of simple fondness? The death threats, potentially beginning around that time. The sudden retirement of the previous curator, though Scarlett was fairly certain that was related to Hershel's declining health. Still, it was a sudden change. She added the usurper notes, Devon's murder, and the disappearance of the mummy.

Scarlett frowned at the paper. She'd hardly begun to list the strange events. The break-in at her house, complete with another usurper note. The attack on Winnie in Scarlett's office. The phone call saying Devon had gotten what he'd deserved. Scarlett made a big star next to that one since she'd almost forgotten it. Peter coming to town and blaming Scarlett for Devon's death. Sayed lying to her. Hershel's collapse in his home. Again, she suspected that was related to his health, but she added it to the mix of horrific incidents.

She read through the list, then tapped the pen against the paper. How was she supposed to make sense of any of it? Scarlett circled the last thing she'd written. She was worried about Hershel. How was he doing? She picked up the landline phone and called the medical center at Crescent Harbor. It was a small facility with only a few beds, so Scarlett had no idea if Hershel was even still there.

She was pleased when the woman who took her call answered her question about Hershel.

"Yes, Hershel Smythe stayed overnight," the woman said, a slight quaver in her voice suggesting she was similar in age to Hershel. "But he'll be transferred today. I don't have a note as to whether that will be to a larger hospital or possibly a care facility."

"Can you tell me when that transfer is going to happen?" Scarlett asked.

"Not until late afternoon," the woman said. Then she chuckled softly. "Anything that involves paperwork always takes a while."

Scarlett thanked her warmly for the information and hung up. She debated if she had time to drive to the medical center before Luke returned her call. She had no idea how long it could take for the wheels of justice to turn.

She slipped her phone into her pocket and made it as far as the hall before running into Max Northrup.

"I've finished the faux rock walls in the special exhibit maze," Max said. "Now I'm wiring the lights for the small display alcoves. Before I get too far into that, I'm going to need you to come and okay them for size. You told me that you didn't have enough details on all the artifacts for that when I first cut them, so I haven't started cleaning up those spaces."

"Of course. Please hold on a moment." Scarlett ducked into her office. Though she'd expected Max to wait outside, he followed her in. She gave him a copy of the artifact list that she'd made as she unloaded crates. She'd noted all the dimensions on the list. "These are the items to house. I also planned to move some of the artifacts already in our permanent Egyptian exhibit to the special exhibit, but we can base how many and which ones on available space."

Max nodded as he scanned the list. "Each of these gets its own alcove?"

"Not necessarily," Scarlett said. "For instance, this set of ushabti would go in the same alcove. They're by the same artist and probably part of the same tomb." She grabbed a pencil and made notes of other items that could be grouped together.

"Let me compare this to what I've done so far," he said. "If there are any problems, I'll let you know."

"Thanks. I appreciate the great work you and Phillip are doing." She grinned. "Especially considering you've been working in the dark a lot."

"It has its challenges," Max admitted. "I'll have to wait until tomorrow to pass your thanks on to Phillip. He called in sick."

Scarlett wasn't overly surprised by that. She wondered if Phillip was staying away from the museum because the police wanted to speak with him about Winnie's attack. At any rate, she didn't want to discuss that with Max. "I hope he feels better soon. Do you need more help?"

He chuckled. "Not for this step. I could do it in my sleep."

Max left the office in cheerier spirits than when he'd entered, so Scarlett considered that a win. She wished it was always true.

With a last glance at her desk, she headed out of the office again. She made it all the way to the lobby before she was stopped, this time by Luke.

"I've come to whisk you away," he said.

"Oh?"

"I assume you want to be in on the search of Sayed's room."

Scarlett stared at him. "You convinced the chief to let you bring me along?"

Luke smiled. "The chief suggested it. He thought you would be the perfect person to recognize if anything in the room could be related to the case."

She was too stunned to speak.

"You can't touch anything," he warned. "You and I will be there mostly as observers. The officers will be doing the search."

"Of course." Scarlett thought about her plan to visit Hershel and resolved to go straight there when she was done with Luke.

When they arrived at the inn, Mary Gamble told them Dr. Kamal wasn't in, but since the police officers had a hastily secured search warrant, she let them into the man's room.

The room was almost obsessively neat with the only personal touches in sight being the cheerful throw pillows on the overstuffed chair and the small vase of flowers in the center of the vintage dresser. As the officers checked drawers and under the mattress, Scarlett became increasingly anxious that they wouldn't discover anything important.

"Found something," Officer Young called from the bathroom.

Scarlett joined the rush to the doorway.

The officer was crouched down in front of the small bathroom vanity. He held up a few pieces of paper enclosed in a plastic bag. "I don't know what they are, but since they were tucked behind the pipes, they're probably what we're searching for."

"May I see?" Luke asked as he pulled on latex gloves.

Officer Young handed over the package.

Luke opened it and slid the papers out. They were folded in half, and when he unfolded them, it was obvious they were official documents.

Scarlett peeked over Luke's shoulder to read them. "That's the original paperwork on the artifacts. They trace the ownership for each piece." She pointed without touching the paper. "There are the two ushabti I tracked, and these papers show that the owner was Devon Reed, not the Egyptian museum."

She felt as if a band had unwrapped from her chest. The papers would prove who owned each artifact without question. As she scanned the list, she saw that more and more of them belonged to Devon. Only a few of the larger pieces were clearly traceable to the museum in Egypt. "Most of the artifacts were meant to be permanent for us," she announced.

"I concur." Luke slipped the pages into the protective plastic and returned the package to Officer Young.

"I need those," Scarlett protested.

"Sorry, but the documents are evidence," Officer Young said as he tucked the package under his arm. "I expect the chief will authorize you to get copies."

"That will do," Scarlett said. "For now."

"I'd say that gives Dr. Sayed Kamal a pretty big motive," Luke concluded. "He was claiming all the artifacts for the museum, but those documents make it plain that most belonged to Devon Reed. That meant Devon was in the way of Sayed's goals."

"That sounds plausible," Officer Young said. "We'll be picking up Dr. Kamal as soon as we locate him. Who would have been in possession of these documents normally?"

"Devon," Scarlett replied without hesitation. "He would have needed them to sail from Egypt with such a valuable collection."

"That's what I thought," Officer Young said. "We'll want to chat with Dr. Kamal. He needs to explain how the papers passed to him from Mr. Reed. I can't think of a legal reason behind this."

With Sayed's room thoroughly searched and the police on the hunt for the Egyptian, Scarlett and Luke left the inn. As they stepped outside, a cool breeze swept by, making Scarlett shiver despite her light blazer.

"We may have a storm coming in," he said. "It can happen suddenly. The Pacific isn't quite as peaceful as the name implies."

"I'm glad I'm not out on the water."

"Do you want to grab some lunch with me?" Luke asked. "We could talk more about the case."

Scarlett was surprised by the invitation. She wasn't sure what more they had to talk about, then remembered she wanted to tell him about the death threats to Devon. However, she had something else she wanted to do first. "Lunch sounds great, but I planned to check on Hershel. I called the medical center while I was waiting to hear from you. They're moving him this afternoon, and I want to see him before that happens."

"If you don't mind, I'll come with you," he said. "I'd like to have a word with him myself."

With that settled, they drove to the medical center.

The receptionist recognized Luke and greeted him warmly. As soon as he said they wanted to see Hershel, she insisted on leading the way.

Scarlett was surprised to realize she found the woman's enthusiasm about Luke more than a little irritating. *What do I care if he charms every woman in Crescent Harbor?*

When they reached the elderly man's room, Scarlett was shocked to see Phillip Bentley standing close to the hospital bed. Her first instinct was to worry about Hershel.

"Wait," Luke whispered to her. "I'll call the police."

Scarlett had no intention of letting Phillip hurt the elderly man, and she rushed in, heedless of Luke's warning. "Mr. Smythe, are you all right?"

"No, he's not," Phillip snapped. "And it's your fault. Get out of my grandfather's room before you do even more damage."

Grandfather? Scarlett felt her mouth hanging open and quickly shut it. Hershel had mentioned he had a grandson, but she'd never guessed it was Phillip. "The police want to speak with you."

"Which is also your fault," Phillip said. "You're the one who told them I attacked Winnie, which I did not. And you're the one who took my grandfather's job and made him sick."

"Phillip!" Hershel scolded. His voice was weak, but it conveyed serious annoyance. "What's this foolishness? You know how to behave better than that."

"You need to rest," Phillip urged, his tone instantly contrite.

"You need to apologize to Scarlett," Hershel said, "because you're all wrong. She didn't take my job. I insisted that Devon find a replacement."

"What?" Phillip asked. "You loved that job."

Hershel closed his eyes for a moment. When he opened them, his voice sounded stronger. "I did, but I was getting sick. I'd put off going to the doctor when I saw that I was losing weight. I suppose I was afraid of what I'd learn. When I got my cancer diagnosis, I told Devon I needed to retire."

The pieces tumbled into place in Scarlett's head. She pointed at Phillip. "You thought I was a usurper."

Phillip nodded, his expression miserable.

"You sent those flowers and the cards," Scarlett continued. "You broke into my home. You called and said Devon got what he deserved. You attacked Winnie. All because you thought I pushed your grandfather out of his job?"

Phillip waved his hands in denial. "I did *not* hurt Winnie. I would never do anything like that. She's a nice person. I found her that way when I went to your office to tell you what I thought of you. I was done playing games."

"Why don't I believe you?" This came from Luke, who had joined them in the room.

"I swear it's true," Phillip insisted. He faced Scarlett. "I asked my girlfriend at the florist to paint chemicals on the flower stems that would make them wilt when mixed with water. I wrote the cards. I went inside your house. I was going to tape the note on the back door, but the door wasn't locked. I didn't break in. I even made the phone call because I thought Devon pushed out my grandfather in favor of someone younger. But I didn't hurt anyone."

"You don't think terrorizing Scarlett was hurtful?" Luke asked, his voice almost dangerously calm.

"I've suffered too," Phillip whined. "My girlfriend broke up with me after the police showed up at the florist to question her. That's when I started to realize all the cloak-and-dagger stuff was stupid and cowardly."

Luke didn't respond, his expression stony.

"I was going to confront you and tell you exactly what I thought of you," Phillip said to Scarlett. "I went to your office, but you weren't there. Winnie was. I tried to help her, and then you showed up. I was aware it looked bad, so I panicked and took off. But I knew you'd take care of Winnie."

"Really?" Scarlett asked, folding her arms over her chest. "You trusted me after thinking I'd pushed your grandfather out of his job?"

Phillip averted his gaze. "Yeah, I did."

Hershel reached out and rested his hand on Phillip's arm. "You've made a grand mess of things, haven't you?"

Phillip blinked. "I guess I have," he told his grandfather, his voice thick with emotion.

"You'll need to tell all of this to the police," Luke said. "They'll want to question you at length."

"What about my grandfather?" Phillip asked.

The older man snorted. "I think I can ride in an ambulance to the hospital without you. But when you get this settled with the police, I expect to see you. We have a lot to discuss."

"Yes, I'll be there," Phillip promised.

Scarlett studied Phillip closely. He sounded genuinely repentant, and his horror about being accused of hurting Winnie sounded true enough.

But after everything he'd just confessed, how could she believe him?

20

Hershel waved away the nurses' attempts to fuss over him.

Scarlett feared that seeing his grandson arrested and taken away in handcuffs couldn't have done his condition any good.

Hershel insisted that he was fine, then crooked his finger at Luke. "Come here."

Luke exchanged glances with a frowning nurse.

Hershel flapped a hand at the woman.

The nurse huffed in exasperation. "Since he's being unreasonable, you may as well do whatever he wants," she told Luke.

He gave her a sympathetic smile and approached the retired curator's bedside.

"Please do what you can for Phillip," Hershel said. "This is my fault. If I hadn't tried to hide my condition from my family, he would never have jumped to those ridiculous conclusions. My pride and secretiveness prompted his behavior."

"I promise all of that will be taken into consideration," Luke said.

Hershel peered into Luke's eyes, clearly assessing his trustworthiness, then slumped on his pillows.

It was obvious that Hershel's plea had taken even more out of him, and Scarlett hurried to his side. "Please let the nurses take care of you."

"Plenty of time for that," Hershel said, though his voice was distinctly weaker. "I'm sorry, my dear."

"It's not your fault," she assured him. "I don't blame you."

"My grandson would never hurt anyone," Hershel said. "Whoever hurt Winnie, it wasn't Phillip."

"I hope not." It was the first lie Scarlett had told him. She actually wished she could believe Phillip *had* knocked Winnie out, because it would mean her attacker was in custody. Though Scarlett strongly hoped that the police would soon find Sayed and announce the man had attacked Winnie and killed Devon.

The elderly man sighed.

Scarlett patted his hand. "No one will try to railroad your grandson. To be honest, I think Winnie's attack was connected to the new exhibit, the one I told you about."

"The Egyptian one?" Hershel asked. He seemed to rally a bit.

Scarlett wasn't sure if she should say anything else, but she suspected it would make the man feel better to think about something other than his grandson in jail. So she explained about Sayed and his false claims that the museum in Cairo owned all the artifacts. "His motivation may have been to return culturally and historically significant objects to Egypt, but sometimes zeal for the right cause can drive a person to do the wrong thing."

"Devon wasn't guilty of cultural misappropriation," Hershel said with conviction. "Many times he sent antiquities he'd acquired to the Egyptian museum when he could tie their origin to a specific tomb. All the objects he kept in his own museum had lost their original connections. They'd been stolen by local tomb robbers and sold to tourists, then sold repeatedly before they ended up in Devon's hands."

"I suppose Sayed would argue that they were still Egyptian," Scarlett said, daring to play devil's advocate simply because the discussion appeared to be making Hershel feel better.

"They were undoubtedly Egyptian," Hershel agreed. "But each piece had lost its ties to history. Returning them would do little good.

Devon always made the collection available to scholars to study styles or pottery glazes, things like that." He slumped a little.

"Thank you for telling me all that," Scarlett said. "Please get some rest."

"I may take a nap before they move me to the hospital in Monterey." Hershel motioned to Luke. "Be sure to keep me updated on Phillip."

"I will," Luke promised.

Scarlett had no idea what would happen to Phillip, but she hoped that Luke would be able to deliver encouraging news for Hershel's sake.

When Scarlett finally returned to the museum, Winnie met her at the lobby door. "You must have been watching for me," Scarlett said, but the chuckle in her voice faded when she noticed Winnie's concerned expression. "What happened?"

Winnie caught Scarlett by the arm and tugged her to follow. "Sayed arrived at the museum after you left. He insisted on waiting in your office, so I sent some security guards to wait with him. That didn't last long. He demanded to be taken downstairs to check on the status of the artifacts."

Scarlett widened her eyes in alarm. "I hope you didn't agree to that."

"I tried to get in touch with you several times," Winnie said, meeting the implied reproof with her own. "But you didn't return my calls. I believe we should phone the police, but I wanted to speak to you first."

Scarlett winced. She'd switched off her phone during the search of Sayed's room at the Harbor View Inn, and she'd left it that way since they were going to be at the medical center, which had posted signs restricting cell phone use everywhere. "Sorry about that. Where is Sayed now?"

"In the storage room," Winnie replied. "My security people are with him, so he can't get up to any mischief, and it seemed like a good way to keep him contained."

Scarlett winced again. She preferred Sayed be kept as far from the artifacts as possible.

Winnie appeared not to notice Scarlett's reaction. "I warned the security guards not to be intimidated by anything Sayed tells them. The museum would take responsibility for anything they had to do to protect the artifacts."

"Good. Call the police and tell Chief Rodriguez that Sayed is here."

"On it." Winnie pulled her cell from her pocket and made the call while they continued across the museum to the basement stairwell.

As soon as Winnie ended the call and slipped the phone into her pocket, she faced Scarlett. "Why are the police searching for Sayed? I thought they released him because they didn't have anything on him."

"They did, but we found proof in his hotel room that he lied about who owned the artifacts in our storage room. The bulk of them belonged to Devon, not the museum in Egypt. And the police want to know why he lied and whether killing Devon could have been part of his plan to steal the artifacts. Now it's your turn to answer a question. Why didn't we take the freight elevator?"

"It's loud." Winnie smiled. "And I like surprise entrances."

Scarlett returned her smile. "Good thinking."

They quietly opened the door from the stairwell, and Scarlett trotted the rest of the way to the storeroom on her toes so her heels didn't ring on the floor. She was relieved to see the two security guards standing close to Sayed.

The man berated the guards for not letting him reseal the crates. "These artifacts are going to Egypt whether you like it or not. You may as well get out of my way."

"Actually," Scarlett said, "they're not."

Sayed spun around and glared at her. "You would dare try to steal from the Egyptian museum?"

"The police found the papers hidden in your room," Scarlett announced. "We know the actual ownership of these artifacts. And so do you."

"They were stolen from Egypt," Sayed argued. "It isn't changed by the fact that Devon Reed wasn't the original thief."

"A past wrong doesn't excuse a present crime," Scarlett said.

"A lie to right a bigger wrong is hardly a crime," Sayed insisted.

"How about murder?" Scarlett asked. "After all, Devon Reed wouldn't have let you get away with this."

"Murder?" Sayed sputtered. "I didn't kill anyone. I merely took advantage of an unfortunate incident to right an old wrong. You must realize I would never be so disrespectful as to remove Usewatu from his coffin."

Scarlett hesitated. That part had made her question Sayed's guilt before. The man was a zealot, but that zeal would surely have prevented him from harming the mummy. "Perhaps you did it for the greater good of keeping him in Egypt. He could have been removed with care before the mummy case was sent to the ship. Usewatu might never have even left Egypt."

Sayed slammed a hand down on the nearest crate. "I won't be accused of this, and I won't be tricked into admitting to a crime I didn't commit."

"Your guilt or innocence isn't mine to decide," Scarlett said. "And your confession or refusal isn't important to me either. The police will decide what to do about that. Now perhaps we should wait for them upstairs."

"Fine," Sayed said with a huff. He shrugged away from the security guards and marched by Scarlett and Winnie, continuing toward the door.

Scarlett felt a wave of relief that he had given in so easily.

Suddenly, Sayed knocked a lid off one of the small crates near the door and grabbed the artifact from inside. It was a small pottery vessel, one of the most beautiful and fragile in the whole collection. Scarlett knew it belonged to Devon.

With the vessel in hand, Sayed bolted for the door.

21

Winnie sprinted after Sayed, and the security guards ducked around Scarlett to join the chase.

"Be careful," Scarlett called after them. "I don't want that artifact damaged. It's irreplaceable."

She followed them out into the basement hallway in time to see one of the guards tackle Sayed.

Scarlett shrieked as the artifact flew out of the man's hands. In that instant, she could picture the priceless vessel smashing to the floor, lost forever.

Winnie lunged and caught the fragile piece mere inches from the concrete floor. The head of security curled around the artifact before she hit the hard floor herself with a grunt.

The second guard ignored Sayed and immediately went to help Winnie.

Sayed wriggled out from under the burly security guard who had tackled him. The guard lunged for Sayed, nearly snagging his leg, but the Egyptian was fast. By the time the guard made it to his feet, Sayed was gone.

"Go after Sayed," Winnie instructed, brushing off the attention of the guard trying to help her.

Though both guards gave Winnie one last concerned glance, they obeyed and rushed down the hall to the stairs.

"Are you all right?" Scarlett asked. "Did you hit your head?"

"No, this time the bruises will be in new places." Winnie held out the pottery vessel. "I don't think it struck the floor, but I'm sure you'll want to check it over."

Scarlett did, shifting the piece to examine it from all sides. It had a few worn cracks, but there were no fresh ones. "It's perfect. You saved the day."

"Only if the guards catch Sayed before he gets away."

Scarlett pointed at her. "I'm the boss here. If I say you saved the day, then you did."

Winnie smiled. "Yes ma'am."

Scarlett groaned. "Anything but 'ma'am.'" She carried the pot to the storeroom and nestled it carefully in the crate. "Let's go upstairs. I expect the police will be here any second to take Sayed into custody."

They climbed the stairs slowly since Scarlett noticed Winnie walked with a slight limp. "Are you sure you're not hurt?"

"Nothing a hot bath won't cure," Winnie answered.

"As soon as we're done with the police, you should go home and have one."

Winnie didn't comment, but Scarlett suspected she wouldn't leave the museum while it was open.

When they reached the lobby, Scarlett spotted the two security guards who'd chased after Sayed. They were speaking with Officers Nina Garcia and James Young. Scarlett wondered what it said about her past week that she now knew the names and faces of several local police officers. *I've spoken to the officers of Crescent Harbor more than all the times I've ever dealt with policemen in my life.* She admired the officers she'd met, but she'd rather see them less often, at least professionally.

"Sorry," one of the security men said as they approached, his face a mask of regret. "The guy got away."

"He knocked aside a woman with one of those baby backpacks," the other guard said, his tone matter-of-fact rather than defensive. "We had to stop and make sure she and the baby were okay."

"Upon reflection, one of us probably should have continued the chase," the first guard said. "But I guess we were both acting instinctively. It was a baby."

"I can understand that," Scarlett said. "Were they all right?"

"The baby was kicking up a fuss," the first guard said. "But he was only scared, not hurt. As soon as I saw that, I went after Sayed again, but he'd already gotten away."

"You both did the right thing," Winnie told them, and her voice didn't hold even a trace of reproof. "Your first responsibility is the safety of the museum patrons and staff."

The guards squared their shoulders, clearly boosted by the support.

Scarlett refocused on the two police officers. "I don't suppose you're going to tell me that you nabbed Sayed outside."

"I'm afraid not," Garcia said. "We were delayed by a traffic accident a few blocks away. We had to see if we needed to render aid. As it happens, no one was injured."

"That's good," Scarlett said. "I assume you've been filled in about Sayed's visit."

"We have," Officer Young said, then addressed Winnie. "Are you okay?"

"Yes," Winnie replied, smoothly deflecting attention from herself. "What is being done to apprehend the suspect?"

"We've been watching his room at the inn," Officer Garcia said.

"But I doubt he'll return there," Young chimed in. "He knows we're onto him and his attempt to scam the museum out of artifacts. I imagine he's searching for a way out of the country. His name has been distributed to airlines and passenger ships. I'm expecting him to head for the harbor, so we'll concentrate our efforts there."

"Why the harbor?" Scarlett asked.

"It's much easier to get aboard a ship than a plane," Garcia explained. "Especially if you're willing to part with some cash."

Scarlett was glad the police had a plan, but she was even more relieved at the thought of not having any more encounters with Dr. Sayed Kamal. Now all she had to do was establish a new connection with the Egyptian museum. Maybe the contact Winnie had given her?

"Miss McCormick?" Officer Young asked.

Scarlett's attention snapped back to the moment. She'd probably missed something. "Yes?"

"I was asking if there was anything else you needed from us," Young said.

"No, I'm good," Scarlett said. "Please let me know if you catch Sayed."

The officers agreed, then walked away.

Scarlett retreated a few steps before heading for the stairs. She needed to make some calls. As she walked, she thought about the wonderful people she'd met during her work trips to Egypt. Overall, she liked and admired the Egyptian people, and she even understood Sayed's passion for keeping Egyptian antiquities in Egypt. Of course, that didn't begin to excuse murder.

When she reached the top of the stairs, the soft sneakered footfalls finally registered in her mind, and by then, Winnie had caught up with her.

"I'm going to have to work on that," Scarlett muttered.

"Work on what?" Winnie asked.

"Getting so single-minded that I miss what's going on around me. The professor who led the first archaeological expedition I was ever on told me that he suspected I'd miss the end of the world if I was busy trying to identify a pottery shard."

"I don't think it's that bad," Winnie said loyally.

Scarlett chuckled. "Actually, he said that because I failed to notice a wild boar breaking into the camp and knocking down a tent while I was sitting at our worktable examining pottery shards."

Winnie grinned. "That's impressive."

"If you've got a minute, I want to catch you up on what we learned from Phillip Bentley," Scarlett said. "Did you know he's Hershel's grandson? He was also the one who sent all the flowers and usurper cards."

Winnie frowned. "I guess that helps explain why he hit me on the head."

Scarlett started walking toward her office with Winnie at her side. "He maintains that he didn't, and I'm inclined to believe him. I assume Sayed was lurking in the office, probably to make sure I didn't have any evidence against him, and hit you when you came in."

"Not my finest moment as a security chief," Winnie said dryly.

Scarlett stopped and smiled at Winnie. "You saved a priceless artifact today. You're my hero."

Winnie held up her hands. "You're the boss." Then she changed the subject. "Do you believe Sayed attacked me and murdered Devon?"

"I don't know," Scarlett said as she resumed walking. "I could see Sayed hitting you. He strikes me as a violent man, but until we find Usewatu, I won't be convinced. If the mummy was safely removed from the case, I'll believe Sayed did it. But finding scattered mummy wrappings on that ship suggests recklessness, and he cares too much about the artifacts for that."

They had reached the doorway to the office, and Scarlett stepped inside.

Winnie didn't follow. Instead, she merely said, "People do desperate things in desperate situations."

Scarlett leaned against the doorframe. "I'm going to call that contact you made at the Egyptian museum. I'll need someone new to handle the situation with the artifacts that *do* belong to them, including Usewatu's case. I want a final ruling on whether we can use them for the special exhibit."

Winnie wrinkled her nose. "I don't envy you dealing with bureaucracy. I'm going to get a cup of coffee, then watch the security tape from the basement. I'm sure the men didn't let Sayed touch anything before we got there, but I want to check."

"Sounds good. But you really should head home early today. I mean it."

Winnie smiled, the corners of her eyes crinkling, and walked away.

Scarlett settled into her battle with bureaucracy. The call to Winnie's contact was considerably less painful than she'd expected. The man had already planned to call Sayed home as soon as he could contact him.

"It won't be quite that easy," Scarlett warned. "Our police want to speak with him."

The man on the other end of the phone sighed. "I have long suspected that Sayed's zealotry would catch up to us all. I will call your authorities and get an update. In the meanwhile, be reassured, the museum will honor our arrangement with Devon Reed. You may exhibit the artifacts before you return them to us."

Scarlett thanked the man warmly and ended the call. It was nice to have something work out without a struggle. But she didn't have much time to bask in the ease of the exchange, because a knock on her open door drew her attention.

Peter stood in the doorway, his expression sheepish. "Do you have a few minutes?"

"It's been a long day," Scarlett said. "If you've come to accuse me of murder, I'll pass. Maybe some other time."

He hung his head. "Allie has already read me the riot act over my wild accusations. So has the chief of police. I have been thoroughly chastened."

She stood. "Good, because I didn't deserve that."

"No, you didn't. Can I come in?"

Scarlett didn't answer immediately. She would have loved to refuse. She felt as if she'd had more than enough on her plate in the last few days, but she remembered that this man was one of Allie's good friends. Her own friendship with Allie probably meant she owed him a short conversation.

"Yes," she said. "But I have work to do, so I can only spare a few minutes."

Peter straightened his shoulders, and his expression lightened a bit. "Allie said you wouldn't hold a grudge."

"Don't count on that," Scarlett said. She waved at the chair across from her. "I can't say I enjoyed being accused of murder."

Peter settled into the chair. "I don't think anyone would. You have to understand my position. I knew virtually everyone at this museum. I knew Hal and Greta wouldn't hurt anyone. Neither would Allie or Winnie or Hershel."

"Got it," she said. "You don't have to name the whole staff, past and present."

"I didn't know you." He shrugged. "Also, I knew this redhead once who had a crazy temper. I think I let that influence my judgment too."

"I suspected you too," Scarlett admitted.

Peter gawked at her in obvious astonishment. "Me? Devon was family."

"A lot of murderers kill family members," she said.

He folded his arms over his chest. "Well, not me. Devon was wonderful to me. He gave me money for a house, even though I was quitting. I mean, that's a great guy."

"Generous certainly," Scarlett said. She had noticed the man's wedding ring when he'd crossed his arms. "I assume Devon approved of your wife."

"Everyone loves Sofia. She's spring sunshine in human form. I've never seen her do an unkind thing."

"The woman who ended up with your old job isn't one of your biggest fans," she remarked.

"Beatrix?" Peter asked. "She's always been sweet whenever I've spoken to her, which is more often than you'd think. I used to call Devon now and then for advice."

"Maybe she was worried you were thinking about taking your job back," Scarlett said. As she thought about it, the young woman's distrust of Peter had been extreme and had gone a long way toward fueling Scarlett's own distrust. Then she remembered something specific Beatrix had said. "She told me Devon was afraid of you."

"Afraid of me?" He laughed. "That's ridiculous."

"Did you hear about Devon's death threats?"

His chuckles abruptly stopped. "Devon was getting death threats?"

"Apparently. He changed his behavior and became more distant and secretive. Christopher Pinchot, a collector he knew, also suggested you could be the source of the threats."

Peter huffed. "Devon was fond of Mr. Pinchot, but I hardly knew the man. I can't imagine why he'd think I threatened Devon. That's crazy."

Once again Scarlett found herself inclined to believe someone's protestation of innocence, and she wondered if she might be gullible. But Peter's warm brown eyes and his earnest tone made it hard to see him in the role of killer.

"I suppose," Scarlett said musingly. "Christopher Pinchot could have gotten the idea from Beatrix too. If so, why would she try to damage your reputation?"

"I knew you'd eventually ask the right question," a voice said from the doorway.

Scarlett froze when she saw Beatrix Morrow there, raising a gun.

22

"I'd rather not shoot anyone," Beatrix said. Any trace of her former wide-eyed innocence was gone.

"Why do I doubt that?" Scarlett asked, trying to sound calm, though she was so frightened that she was having trouble breathing.

Beatrix shrugged. "Believe it. Guns are messy, and I don't need more messy situations. However, I will do what I must if you force me to." She stepped into the office and closed the door behind her.

Scarlett marveled at the change in the previously pleasant woman. "You killed Devon Reed."

"She did?" Peter asked.

Beatrix sneered. "Yes, I did."

His face darkened. "Why?"

Beatrix shrugged. "Killing him wasn't the plan, but plans don't always go smoothly. The key to success is to be ready to improvise."

"How did you know how to write the hieroglyphics on the note you left with Devon?" Scarlett asked. "How did you find out about the notes I was already getting?"

"I copied the hieroglyphics from a book of Devon's." Beatrix grinned. "I had no idea you were getting notes. Isn't coincidence wonderful?"

Peter began to rise from the chair.

Beatrix aimed the gun at him. "Sit down. Are you in a hurry to die?"

He sat down. "If you're going to kill us anyway, what does it matter?"

"Because I have a story to tell," Beatrix growled. "And if you insist on being a nuisance, I'll dispatch you first."

"Tell us your story," Scarlett said. "Explain why you killed a good man."

"A good man?" Beatrix repeated, then laughed. "Maybe you'll feel differently when you hear the truth about him."

Scarlett waved a hand for Beatrix to continue, hoping for a nonchalance she didn't feel.

Beatrix scowled at her, but she began her tale anyway. "Picture this. Nearly thirty years ago, Devon Reed makes an impulsive marriage to a beautiful, if rather naive, woman in London. They were caught up in the bright bloom of love at first sight."

"I assume it didn't go well," Scarlett said.

Beatrix snorted. "It took them only three weeks to realize they had nothing in common and no desire to find common ground. They dissolved the marriage. The woman had no interest in Devon's money, but he insisted on giving her a rather large sum. I imagine he felt guilty about the whole thing."

"Or he was simply an upstanding man who'd made a mistake," Peter said fiercely.

"Whatever." Beatrix rolled her eyes dramatically. "Devon was never told that he'd left the woman with more than money. She was pregnant. She raised the child on her own. They weren't poor, thanks to Devon's largesse, but they weren't nearly as rich as they should have been. An auto accident killed the mother and nearly killed her teenage daughter."

"A tragedy," Scarlett said.

"I suppose," Beatrix said. "At any rate, the teenager healed and completed her schooling. Then she went in search of her father to get the money she deserved."

"I see who the daughter was," Scarlett said.

"I'm not surprised," Beatrix said. "However, you've been remarkably easy to fool so far. I considered announcing who I am, but I wasn't sure how Devon would react. I watched him from a distance, and I started sending him death threats to put him on edge."

"You should have told him," Peter said. "He would have done right by you."

Beatrix snorted. "Why would he do the right thing now when he didn't all those years ago? I chose not to take the risk. My big break came when you quit. Devon was pitifully sad once you were gone. I charmed him into a job easily enough and started stealing from him. I was so guileless and innocent, and he was more than willing to believe I was simply making a few mistakes as I learned the job."

"By then you must have realized Devon wasn't the type to ignore his own child," Peter said.

"You think so?" Beatrix asked, fury crackling in her voice. "He'd never checked up on his ex-wife, never made sure things were well. Never bothered to find out I existed. He'd have known I was there if he cared. But no, it was out of sight, out of mind."

"That's not fair," Scarlett said.

Beatrix laughed. "Life isn't fair. Hasn't anyone ever told you that?"

"You killed your own father," Scarlett responded.

"He was never a father to me," Beatrix said. "But you're rushing the story. As the faithful assistant, I continued right up until the day Devon was due to sail. For some reason, that's the day he decided to wise up."

"He figured out that you were stealing from him," Scarlett said.

Beatrix shook her head. "But he did discover I was sending the death threats."

"Why would you do that?" Scarlett asked.

"To isolate him from everyone and everything he loved," Beatrix explained. "Obviously. And it worked. He gallantly stayed as far away as possible from the museum to keep everyone here safe. It was only the opportunity for this magnificent exhibit that made him willing to risk a trip. Even then, he tried to keep his travel plans a secret, which worked perfectly for me. Well, until he fired me and threatened me with legal action if I ever came near him again. I couldn't have that."

"You poisoned him," Scarlett said.

"By proxy." Beatrix shrugged, as if she'd had no choice. "I was prepared for the possibility that Devon would have to die. I had purchased a supply of venom."

"That's monstrous," Peter said.

"I didn't do any of this for your approval. I wanted my due." Beatrix waved the gun in his direction, then focused on Scarlett. "I can see those wheels turning. You want to know how I got him and the note into the mummy case. Was I secretly on the ship? Am I much stronger than I appear? No. I paid one of the crew a ridiculous amount of money to kill Devon with an injection of the snake venom and prepare the dramatic reveal. He did rather well, and he even saved the mummy for me. The plan was rather improvised, but it worked."

"Then why come here at all?" Scarlett asked.

"I had to make it clear I was still his assistant," Beatrix said. "I doubted he'd told anyone about firing me, and I needed to be sure the fake will I'd created rather brilliantly stood up in court. He gave his sweet little assistant such a lovely parting gift." She batted her eyelashes at Peter. "Much bigger than yours."

"You had nothing to do with Dr. Sayed Kamal?" Scarlett asked.

"Actually, I did," Beatrix said. "I convinced him that I sympathized with his cause, and I suggested the scheme to get all the artifacts. I even talked him into searching your office so I'd know what you might have figured out. But he found nothing, and his attack on your head of security heated everything up."

"You were going to let Sayed keep all the artifacts?" Scarlett asked.

Beatrix snorted. "Hardly. I had some buyers, and I would have eliminated him on the return voyage to Egypt." She narrowed her eyes at Scarlett. "But you ruined it."

Scarlett felt that the breaking point for Beatrix was coming, but the young woman clearly loved the sound of her own voice. "Didn't Sayed mind that you'd committed murder?"

"I'm not stupid," Beatrix said. "He didn't know. I doubt he even suspected such an innocent creature as me. He only cared about getting those artifacts to Egypt."

Scarlett tried to think of something else to ask the woman. She knew whatever happened after Beatrix's story would be bad. She scanned the room, thinking. Over Beatrix's shoulder, Scarlett noticed the door to the office slowly opening.

Peter must have seen it too and decided to play for time. "You monster!" he shouted at Beatrix. "You killed my dearest friend. No, more than that. Devon Reed was like a father to me."

"Too bad he wasn't like a father to me." Beatrix took a step away from him, lining up the barrel of the gun with his forehead.

The door to the office opened enough for Scarlett to see Winnie slip in with her security baton in her hand.

Unfortunately, the traitorous door creaked, and the sound made Beatrix whirl around to face the door—and Winnie.

The young woman would shoot Winnie without hesitation. Scarlett had to do something. She glanced past the phone on her desk and spotted the heavy glass paperweight. She snatched it up and threw it as hard as she could.

The paperweight clocked Beatrix squarely on the head, and she stumbled.

Winnie expertly knocked the gun from Beatrix's hand with the baton.

Then Sayed stormed into the room and seized Beatrix by the shoulder, shaking the woman like a doll. He was bellowing something in Egyptian, and given his tone, Scarlett doubted it was complimentary.

Scarlett, Winnie, and Peter had to intervene to separate Sayed and Beatrix.

As Scarlett phoned the authorities, Peter and Winnie went into action. Peter shoved Sayed down on the sofa and loomed over him, and Winnie dragged Beatrix to a chair and stood over her with the baton.

They stayed that way until the police arrived.

Two weeks later, outside the special exhibits room on the second floor of the Reed Museum of Art and Archaeology, a small crowd lined up, murmuring excitedly.

The slightly spooky Egyptian exhibit had proven to be a hit far beyond Scarlett's most optimistic hopes. She watched the guests from her office doorway and hoped Devon Reed would have been pleased.

She was grateful to Devon. He'd given her an incredible job. He'd left the museum well cared for through a foundation he'd set up. That was why the museum hadn't been mentioned in his real will, to say nothing of the one Beatrix had forged. "I never should have doubted him," she murmured.

"I believe Devon would forgive you," Luke said. "Especially with all you've done to bring the museum to this special day."

Scarlett raised an eyebrow at Luke, wondering if he had read her mind. Then she realized she must have been musing aloud. "It helps that you found Usewatu."

"I'm only sorry that my brainstorm about that took me away from the museum the day Beatrix tried to kill you," he said. "I shouldn't have left your side after we recovered those papers from Sayed's room."

"I neither expect nor need a bodyguard," Scarlett insisted with a sniff.

"I'm not so sure about that," Luke said.

"Because you don't know me."

"Hopefully, we'll fix that," he said with a grin. "At least it ended well. Beatrix was arrested for murder. Sayed is being held while the powers that be figure out whether to charge him for the assault on Winnie or simply ship him back to Egypt to face justice there. In a fruitless effort to deflect blame from herself, Beatrix even identified the man who murdered Devon at her request. And the lab has confirmed that the injection was made into one of the wounds he got from a scuffle with the man. Devon was a fighter to the end."

Scarlett felt her eyes sting. She wished she'd known Devon better. To distract herself, she added to Luke's litany. "We also know that it was the newest security man who let Sayed into the museum when it was closed. He finally confessed and faced the scolding. I think he was grateful not to lose his job. Also, I've heard that Hershel has enrolled in a clinical trial for a new treatment for his condition. He and Phillip are very hopeful." She gave Luke an especially warm smile. "Thank you for helping to keep Phillip out of jail."

"You're the one who didn't press charges," Luke reminded her.

"I do have one more question," she said. "How did the snake get inside the crate?"

"That mystery was solved when they arrested the crewman," he replied. "Beatrix sent along a snake in case the killer needed more venom. The man was less than thrilled at the risk of being caught with a deadly snake, so he dumped it in a crate and nailed it up. He told the police Beatrix was crazy for thinking he'd milk venom from a snake."

"It's obvious that she's mentally unstable for a lot of reasons," Scarlett said. "Tell me more about your brainstorm, the one that helped you locate Usewatu."

"We knew the mummy wasn't on the ship," Luke said. "The police assumed it was tossed overboard. But in my experience, something that valuable isn't discarded lightly. I also knew it wouldn't exactly fit in a duffel bag. I tracked all the crates that were unloaded before the police seized the ship. Only one ended up in a storage facility in Monterey."

"Poor Usewatu," she said. "He was put through a lot. I'm a little surprised the Egyptian museum has been so understanding."

"I'm sure they're embarrassed over Sayed's behavior," he said. "After all, they sent him."

"I don't feel sorry for him, but I do admire his passion for his people's history. And I believe he never intended to keep the antiquities for himself."

"Sayed made his bed when he hid the paperwork Beatrix's hired killer stole from Devon's body," Luke said. "He never even asked how she'd come upon the papers. He was blinded by his own zealotry. Also, Beatrix probably intended to kill him, so he's better off than he could have been."

"True," Scarlett said. "So much of what happened was spurred by passion overruling common sense. Beatrix's fury and sense of entitlement started it. Phillip's love for his grandfather made him believe terrorizing me was right. And Sayed's passion led him to ignore all the warning signs and throw in with a killer."

"That's the problem with passion," he said. "If it's not tempered, it can overrule all common sense. That's why I prefer not to lose myself to emotion."

Scarlett wondered if there was a story behind his last comment, but she didn't know Luke well enough to ask about it. She didn't want to damage the friendship she thought they were developing. As she realized she'd made another friend in Crescent Harbor, she smiled. This town was good for her.

"What's brought on the smile?" he asked.

"I'm glad I live here now," she said. Then the glow faded a little. "But I'm so sorry we lost a good man. I wanted to know Devon more."

"He was worth knowing," Luke agreed. "He would have liked you a great deal. I feel certain you're going to do Devon's legacy proud."

Scarlett wouldn't argue with that. She lifted her chin. "I'm going to do my best."